HAPPILY EVEN AFTER

Lena Matthews

BLUE ISLAND
PUBLIC LIBRARY

Chapter One

"Here we go again," Creigh De Luca muttered to herself as she slipped open the door to her hybrid and climbed out. She stood in the open doorway of her car and brought her hand up to the base of her forehead. Shielding her eyes from the bright glare of the sun, she stared longingly at the door of her ex-husband's house.

It never failed. Whenever it was time for her to drop the kids off for one of their visits with Dean, Creigh begin to feel the waves of what-ifs wash upon her shore of doubts once more. But as usual, she kept her thoughts to herself. What good would it do to admit that the person who had initiated divorce proceedings was the one who wished she could take it all back?

There were no do-overs for life-changing fuckups. So Creigh was learning the hard way to lie in the bed she'd made. After taking a few cleansing breaths, she rounded her car and opened her trunk to take out the duffel bags the kids had packed for their visit.

As a trio the three of them made their way up the walkway to Dean's house. The two kids were laughing and joking around as Creigh fought the urge to smooth down her shoulder-length dark brown hair once more in a lame attempt at vanity. Instead she used her nervous energy to ring the doorbell.

After a few seconds Dean opened the door, meeting them with a big smile aimed directly at Harlow and Hamilton and not an inch higher so there would be no way Creigh could have the mistaken impression he was happy to see her. But that was okay. She was learning to deal with his indifference because the truth of the matter was, despite their problems, Dean was the best dad in the world.

It always warmed Creigh's heart to observe his reaction at seeing the kids after a week away from them. Dean loved their daughter and son with a fierce devotion that made a fatherless woman like Creigh envious and proud all at the same time. Her children were very lucky to have Dean as their father.

Hamilton, putting his well-earned nickname to good use, began to ham it up right away. Standing as rigid as possible, he saluted his father and spoke in a soldier dialect. "Sir, time for changing of the guards, sir."

Dean saluted back before reaching out and then running his hand over the tightly coiled curls of their son's golden brown hair. "At ease, soldier. New LEGOs are on the bed. Why don't you march up there and check them out? We have a storm trooper that needs assembling this weekend, soldier."

"Yes, sir." He saluted once more, then turned on the balls of his tiny feet and lifted his lips up for a kiss, causing Creigh to smile. Beneath the dirt he purposely smudged on his freckled light brown cheeks was the little boy who still preferred she cut the crust off his sandwiches and hadn't quite reached the age where cuddling with his mom was gross. "Bye, Mom."

"Have fun, sweetie. Call me."

"If I get leave to."

Creigh rolled her eyes. "See that you do, Hambone." Hamilton gave a stiff nod of his head, then ran into Dean's house. As she watched him go, Creigh shook her head.

The seven-year-old, who was in his usual weekend wear of fatigues, was taking his soldier obsession a bit far, but Dean, being the type of dad he was, played along with it. He insisted it was perfectly normal. He said at one time or another, all little boys wanted to be soldiers, cowboys, and magicians. Be that as it may, it didn't mean she had to like it. If Creigh had to pick a phase out of all of them, she would have gone with the magician. A cleaner, less violent obsession.

"He is so weird," Harlow muttered, put out with her brother as all big sisters across the universe were from time to time. There wasn't a doubt in Creigh's mind Harlow would take a sucker down for looking at Hamilton the wrong way, but she considered it her sisterly prerogative to give him as much crap as possible. She had two years of superior living on him, which in her mind made her the queen of all things. In Hamilton's mind, she was just a big know-it-all. "I think therapy might be something the two of you should consider for him in the future."

"Thank you, Dr. Phil." Smiling, Dean pulled his daughter in for a hug. The preteen fit just right in the nook of his arms, her head barely coming up to the middle of his chest. "Hey, princess. Missed you."

"Missed you too, Dad." Pulling back, she smiled and peered up at him, her pretty hazel eyes lit with happiness. "Did my Netflix movies arrive?"

"Yes, and the pizza should be here in twenty."

"And you ordered me my own, right? Organic veggies only?" Harlow was going through a PETA-loving health kick that was driving Creigh's food bill up and her patience down. She just couldn't win. One kid wanted to defend the world, and the other wanted to hug it. Creigh supposed it could have been worse, but she was sure stranger stages were ahead.

"Yes. No past lives, flavor, or anything remotely edible shall be on your pizza."

"Perfect." After bouncing over to Creigh, Harlow gave her a quick hug and kiss before following behind her brother into Dean's house. No matter how often she'd come here to either pick up the kids, drop them off, help out with something or the other, Creigh could not get herself to call it anything but Dean's house. The kids' home was with her. Keeping that in mind was the only thing that kept her sane as she roamed her lonely house when it was his time with them. The one thing holding her together.

As soon as Harlow's bouncing russet curls were out of sight, the smile on Dean's face slipped away, and he brought the door toward him as if he were liable to shut it at any time. He instantly became closed off, putting up a wall that clearly read *hands off.* A year hadn't changed much between the two of them. He was still angry and felt wronged, and she was still sad and felt wronged. And as the old saying went, two wrongs didn't make a right. "Same plan as last week. Your house, Sunday night, before six."

"Yes." The one bright spot of her weekend. The day her kids came back home.

"Okay, then." Dean began to close the door.

"Wait," she called out, willing her courage to rise. "I…ummm…I need to talk to you." It was now or never.

"Talk to"—Dean glanced around him in disbelief before facing her once more—"me. I thought the only talking we did was with lawyers."

"That was months ago," she bit out. *Will this ever get easier?*

"Funny, it feels like just yesterday."

Creigh felt her temper flare. "How long are you going to keep holding the divorce against me?"

"Until it stops hurting."

"Apparently this is not the time to talk." She took a step back. Breaking the news to him when he was in a mood like this would only make things worse. "I'll try back another time."

Cursing under his breath, Dean stepped out of the house and closed the door behind him. "Another time? This must be important if you're trying to pencil in time to talk to me."

It was, and the longer she waited, the harder it would be to tell him. "I wouldn't be talking to you if it wasn't."

He hesitated for a moment. "Is it about the kids?"

Creigh nodded. "It involves them, yes."

"Okay." Dean turned around and opened the door wide, waving her in. She did her best to walk past him without contact, but her efforts weren't enough, and they touched for a brief moment. As short of a time as it was, Creigh shouldn't have even noticed, let alone been affected by it. But she was. Her sensitive nipples instantly tightened beneath her shirt, a telltale sign if there was any, of the longing she still felt for this irresistible man.

Maybe it was because it had been far too long since she felt the weight of a man against her. Maybe it was because her hormones were overriding her brain. Or maybe it was simply because Dean was the best lover she'd ever had. No matter, it was damn near impossible for Creigh to be in the same room with him and not feel a tug of desire for him.

Dean's quick intake of breath let Creigh know she wasn't the only one affected. But before she could think of the implications of what that might mean, he stiffened and pulled back. Mortified, she hastened her steps and moved away from him. Good Lord. She had to get herself together before she made a fool out of herself.

She transferred her attention from her ex to her surroundings instead. His home was smaller than the one they'd lived in when they'd been together, but still comfortable enough to accommodate the kids when they visited. A word he despised.

"Mom?" Harlow's hazel eyes widened when she spotted Creigh.

Creigh shot her a quick smile, but it was Dean who spoke. "Your mom and I need to talk. Go check on your brother, and the two of you stay upstairs until I come and get you."

"Why?" Her gaze darted between her parents. "What's going on?"

"Adult stuff that has nothing to do with you. Now get." He punctuated his words with a playful swat to her behind. Harlow started up the stairs, but she continued to glance back over her shoulder in curiosity. When she was out of sight, he turned to face Creigh again. "Let's go in the kitchen."

"Okay," she said, following behind him when he went into the other room. As they walked she ran her gaze over him, taking in his outfit. He was dressed in what Creigh lovingly called De Luca wear. The staple clothing of all the De Luca men in Dean's immediately family—jeans and T-shirt with another shirt on top. And although his brothers made the very causal outfit look good, on Dean it was a work of art. Unable to help herself, she dropped her gaze to his ass, framed nicely by the faded denim he wore like a second skin.

The unbuttoned green long-sleeved shirt he sported over his black T-shirt had seen better days, but it suited him to a tee. Dean was in no way metrosexual. He'd never met a cotton T-shirt he didn't love and thought nothing about using his shampoo as body wash and face cleanser. He was a simple man with simple pleasures, yet he never failed to make her heart skip a beat. Even now, after all this time and with everything that had gone down between them, Creigh couldn't look away. Her sex throbbed at the mere sight of him.

Stop it, she ordered herself. Creigh needed to get herself together and fast, before she began to hump his leg like horny little Chihuahua.

By the time they entered the kitchen, Creigh had her libido back under control. As usual, Dean pulled out the chair for her, as was his custom. It was a testament to his upbringing that he still was chivalrous even when she knew he didn't want her around. "Have a seat."

Without speaking, she complied, then watched, disheartened, as he moved past the table and leaned against the kitchen counter, putting as much space between them as the small room allowed. *Has it really come to this?*

"So is this the part of the divorce where we become buddies? Are you going to start hooking me up with your single friends now that the ink is dry?"

"If I recall correctly, you didn't need the ink to be dry before you started hooking up." The accusation was out before she could help it, but some wounds took longer to heal.

Dean's mouth set into a hard line. "We were separated and *you* left *me*, if you recall correctly."

There was nothing wrong with her memory or apparently his rebound skills. "And a man has his needs."

"Yeah, the need to feel like a man and not like a failure just happens to be one."

"I never said you were a failure." She never even thought it.

"You left me. I think we can pretty much chalk that up as a fail."

She might have been the one to file the papers, but she wasn't the one who left. Dean had checked out of their marriage emotionally a long time before she'd sought a lawyer. "Everything isn't so black or…" Creigh closed her eyes and took another deep breath. This wasn't getting them anywhere. It was also why their changing of the guard happened on doorsteps and in public places. They still hadn't managed to recover from the bitter feelings of the divorce to act like adults quite yet. Releasing the breath, Creigh opened her eyes and forced her lips to tilt up in a smile. She would be civil if it killed her. "I didn't come here to fight with you. I came to talk."

"Talk." Dean snorted. "Not exactly our strong suit," he reminded her unnecessarily. He was right, though. There had been a lot of things they'd been good at, bed being number one, and talking being dead last.

"Then let's pretend to be other people for today. Adult people."

The corner of his lips turned upward. "That's not fun."

"Be that as it may, it's what I need today."

"I'm surprised you're coming to me with a need. I figured I would be last on the list of people you'd turn to."

"You'd figure wrong. We were friends a long time before we were lovers and for a much longer time than we were actual lovers." Creigh glanced down at her hands. "Sometimes I think we should have just stayed friends, but then of course there'd be no Harlow, no Hamilton."

"And that would be unbearable."

She glanced up and nodded. On that they could agree. "Yes, it would. It's also in their name and the name of our former friendship that I want to venture out on this limb and talk to you about something."

"Is there something wrong?"

"Not entirely." There was never going to be a better opening than this. "I'm pregnant."

Dean's head jerked back as if her words assaulted him. "Pre-pregnant. Are you sure?"

"As sure as three pregnancy tests, two sonograms, and several bouts of morning sickness can be." She tried to infuse some lightness in her voice to downplay the tension that filled the room.

"Damn." Dean paled, and he dropped lifelessly into the chair in front of her. Gone was the condescending man who opened his house to her just minutes earlier, and in his place was someone who appeared as if he just had his world kicked out from under him. It was a feeling Creigh knew well. "That's pretty pregnant."

"Yes, it is."

"Is this your way of telling me you're getting"—the final word seem to stick in his throat, making Creigh wonder if, like her, he had a hard time accepting the fact they were completely divorced—"remarried."

"No." Marriage was so not in the cards. "This is my way of telling you I'm pregnant."

His fingers clenched into a fist, and his voice became tense. "And the father?"

Creigh wanted so badly to remind Dean it took more than a donation to make a man a father, but she refrained. That was her own heartbreak she'd have to learn to deal with. It wasn't his fault or problem. So instead, she tried to play off her anger at her stupidity and shrugged as if it meant nothing. "What about him?"

"What's his role in all this?"

"He's not going to have a role." Something she was becoming more and more okay with the longer she had to deal with it.

His hazel eyes narrowed. "Your call or his?"

Creigh avoided his gaze. She didn't want to lie to him, but there was no way she could tell him the truth. "Let's just say it's mutual."

"Mutual." Creigh could see the very idea of a man not wanting to take part in his child's life was so foreign to Dean it was laughable. Dean was raised to take responsibility for his actions, to be a man at all costs, and never to fail. Personally, she always thought his upbringing played a large part in the hostility between the two of them now thanks to the divorce. "Not everyone wants to be a father."

"Then he should have worn a condom. Or you should have been on birth control. Why weren't you? God, Creigh, how could you be so stupid?"

Creigh felt herself begin to tense up. "I don't need a safe-sex lecture from you."

"Apparently not. It would be a bit like shutting the barn door after the cow escaped."

"And I damn sure don't need you passing judgment on me," she snapped.

Dean's eyes flashed with anger. His jaw was rigid, and Creigh knew he was doing everything he could to keep his temper in check. After a few seconds of silence, he looked at her again. "So what are you going to do?"

"What do you think I'm going to do?" For her, there had never been a question.

"You're going to have it."

Creigh let out a sigh. She'd done so many things wrong. Slept with a man she didn't care about in hopes of jump-starting a lagging libido and boosting her self-esteem after seeing Dean out on a date with a younger, thinner, paler woman. Her pity party resulted in a night she wished she could forget with a jerk she wished she'd never met, but also a surprising little gift nuzzled right under her heart. No matter the circumstances of the baby's creation, it still was Creigh's baby. "Yes. I'm going to have her."

"Her. You know the sex already?" His gaze lowered to her barely-beginning-to-thicken waist, hidden quite well beneath the loose-fitting shirt she wore. "How far along are you?"

"Four and a half months," she admitted reluctantly.

"Four and a hal—" Dean erupted from his chair. "Why did you wait so long to say something?"

Warily, Creigh watched him storm over to the sink and grasp the front in his large, strong hands, holding on as if his very life, or hers, depended on it. "Superstitious, I guess. I needed to pass the three-month milestone before I could even begin to think of telling everyone. Announcing a pregnancy is easy, but *un*announcing one is a whole other ballgame." A fact they both knew well after their miscarriage three years earlier.

"Do the kids know yet?" he asked without turning back around to face her.

Creigh shook her head even though she knew he couldn't see her. "No. I wanted to tell you first. I know it's not going to be easy for them." Hell, it still wasn't easy for her, but nothing worthwhile ever was. "Harlow, especially. She's never given up on the idea of us reconciling. And of course it doesn't help she thinks you walk on water."

Dean glanced over his shoulder at her. "I'm not exactly thinking Christlike thoughts right now."

"You'd be a saint if you were." And a saint he wasn't. No one knew that better than her. But her wavering feelings for him had nothing to do with the immediate problem at hand. "This is going to hurt them at first, confuse them even, but in time they'll adapt. Kids do."

"Adapt." Dean crossed his arms over his chest and turned around to face her once more. Anger clouded his features. Fury filled his voice. "Isn't that the line you fed me when you decided we should split up?"

Decide. He made it seem as if making the choice to ask him to leave was as easy as picking out an outfit to wear. It had been the hardest thing she'd ever had to do. Even harder than sitting before the man she still loved and having him stare at her as if she were branded with a scarlet *A* on her breast. But it had been the right thing to do. They'd been drowning, coming apart at the seams, and it was all she could do to stay afloat.

Dean was a stickler for seeing something to the end, and Creigh was afraid his need to make the best of the situation would have torpedoed the thin strand of friendship they had left. If she couldn't have his heart, at the very least she wanted his friendship. But even that seemed to be asking for too much.

She tried again to be civil. "If you could make this a little less difficult for me, I wouldn't hold it against you."

"I'm sorry if I'm not handling this as well as you'd like. It's not every day a man finds out his wife is pregnant with another man's child."

"Ex-wife."

"Thanks for the reminder," he said bitterly.

"You're very welcome." Creigh ran her hand across her eyes and sighed. *God, could this go any worse?* Tired, she folded her hands together in her lap and looked up at him. "It wouldn't kill you to be a bit kinder."

"And would it have killed you to keep your legs closed?" She gasped at his words, and he immediately looked contrite. "I'm... Fuck." Dean spun away from her, but not before Creigh saw the look of disgust on his face.

Shaken, she rose unsteadily to her feet and placed a sheltering hand against her stomach. "And on that note, I'll say good-bye."

Dean turned back to her. "No. Wait. I didn't—"

"I just wanted you to hear it from me," she interrupted, unable to handle much more of his disdain. "I'll see you Sunday night."

Dean let out a heavy sigh. "Creigh."

"Just...don't." Shaking her head, Creigh turned and walked from the room, head held high, holding on to what little pride she had left.

* * *

The early dusk of the evening hadn't turned the night sky completely dark yet, but Dean still needed the lights of his garage to see what was going on under the hood of his 1967 Chevy Impala. Of course, seeing the engine didn't mean it was running any better than it did the last time he tinkered with the car. It was definitely a work in progress. One that helped put his mind at ease, at least for a while. It also kept him from doing something stupid like driving over to his old house and forcing Creigh to tell him the name of the man who'd dared to touch her. All Dean needed was a name. The rest he could find out for himself. And once he did, Dean would make that slimy bastard pay for ever looking in Creigh's direction.

It was bad enough the lowlife had made love to Creigh and impregnated her, but then to have him refuse to step up to the plate was something Dean just could not abide. And he hated like hell that Creigh had to.

Man, she'd looked tired. Her beautiful brown eyes, normally so expressive and full of life, had been dull, lifeless even. Her mocha-tinged skin was far from glowing.

Pregnancy had never been something she'd taken to well, and it didn't appear as if the third time was going to be the charm either. Yet despite the bags, the dull eyes, and the paling brown skin, there was something about her that took his breath away.

That was no real surprise, though. To him Creigh was, hands down, the most beautiful woman to ever walk the earth. She always had been, and Dean knew she would always be to him. She was the mother of his children, his childhood sweetheart, the woman he compared every other woman to, even now when he went out on dates.

No matter who was sitting across from him, they all paled in comparison. Blondes did absolutely nothing for him. Back in the day, before they became what they were now, Creigh used to tease him about how she'd ruined him for all other women. That once he went black, he'd never go back. He'd be damned if she wasn't correct. But it wasn't just black women in general. It was his black woman he wanted. The one who had the nerve to share her body, the body he still considered his, with someone else.

Dean released a pent-up breath and tightened his grip on the ratchet, giving the tool an extra torque just to relieve a bit of the tension bottled inside him. The move didn't help, though. Just as the hole he punched in the kitchen wall after she'd stormed out didn't make him feel better. Nothing short of burying her former lover six feet under would.

The shine of headlights heading up his driveway pulled Dean from his murderous thoughts. He lifted his head to stare around the edge of the sleek black car. Dean immediately recognized his older brother Gino's silver SUV and groaned. Love his siblings as he did, there wasn't a week that went by he didn't regret moving onto a block where two of them owned homes. Boundaries weren't something De Lucas understood very well.

Standing, Dean placed the tool back in its correct slot, then grabbed a rag and wiped the grease from his hands. He shoved the smudged cloth in his back pocket and waited until the older man turned off the engine to his truck and stepped out before greeting him.

"What are you doing here?" he asked in lieu of a customary greeting. It was family. He didn't have to be polite.

"I was driving home and saw you fiddling around with this old wreck, so I stopped by." Gino strolled toward him with a cocky, know-it-all grin on his handsome face. A face that had been on the receiving end of way too many brawls, stitches, and kisses, and left the handsome boxer with scars, trick joints, and a nose broken too many times to count. All factors which fed into Gino's overbearing personality. Gino never met a conversation he hadn't had a comment on. And he never understood some things weren't his business. He was old-school in a lot of ways, and if it involved any member of his family, then it was his business too. "You never mess with this thing unless you're trying to work something out in your mind."

Gino knew him so well, but that didn't mean Dean was going to admit it. His problems were his own, especially when they were of this caliber. "Nothing is on my mind except finally getting this baby running." Dean patted the Impala lovingly.

"Lies. You want to try again?"

There was nothing he wanted to try less. Ignoring his brother, Dean walked back to the open hood and peered in again.

"Well?" Gino followed him, much to Dean's dismay. "You want to tell me what's wrong?"

"I have no idea what you're talking about." Dean gestured to the toolbox behind Gino. "Hand me the open-end wrench."

"You don't need a wrench; you need an exorcist for this piece of shit," Gino grumbled as he did as Dean asked.

"All she needs is a little love." And fifty grand to help cover the things love didn't.

"And you need to learn to talk to people when you're upset and not come out here and play with your toys."

"While I'm learning that, will you be learning how to mind your own business?"

"I already do know how. I just choose not to."

"There's a surprise," Dean muttered under his breath as he began to work anew on his first love. Gino allowed Dean to putter around under the hood for a few grateful minutes before he began to beat the dead horse again.

"Help me out here, little brother. What's today?"

"Friday." Dean couldn't see the trap, but he knew it was coming.

"The kids here?"

"Yes. They're inside watching TV." And thankfully behaving. Unlike their Uncle Gino, though, the kids knew better than to bother him when he was working on his car.

Gino gave a self-satisfied snort. "That explains it, then."

"Explains what?"

"The mood. The ex-Mrs. strikes again."

"You're way off base."

"Doubtful. Even after all this time, she can still push your buttons."

Dean stiffened. "I have no feelings about Creigh in any way, shape, or form." Dean walked over to his toolbox and fiddled around with it for a moment, trying to get his bearings. Maybe if he stayed over here long enough, Gino might get the hint and head home.

"Right." Gino snorted and headed over to the small refrigerator Dean had set up in the garage and grabbed two bottles of beer. "Want one?"

Fuck. He wasn't going away.

Instead of taking it right away, Dean weighed the pros and cons. Pro, a beer. Con, an opening Gino would use to grill him. But that was something he was probably going to do anyway, so Dean took the beer, needing the alcohol to dull his senses and make his brother's words even less memorable.

Gino opened the bottle of beer and leaned back against the Impala. "Do you want to tell me what Creigh did that has you in such a snit?"

Dean took a deep drink, then set the bottle on the hood of the car. "She didn't do anything." *Except fuck some other man.*

"She came by. Obviously that was enough to send you out here to the pit of despair."

"As usual you don't know what you're talking about, not that it stops you from yapping your gums. I'm just out here working on my car. End of story."

"If only that was the case. These days it seems you only work on the beast when you've had a run-in with Creigh."

"You're full of shit."

"I'm not the only one who's noticed. Serge's noticed too."

Dean rolled his eyes. His wet-behind-the-ears brother knew even less about jack crap than their elder brother did. "Well why didn't you say so? Sergio said something. It must be law."

"Don't go discounting the brat just because he's younger."

"He doesn't know his ass from his elbow."

Gino laughed. "True, but Serge doesn't miss much. And now he's working over there with her at the flower shop—"

"Whoa." Dean's head snapped back. "Wait up. Say that again."

"You didn't know?"

"No." Dean snatched his bottle up. *What the hell was that all about?*

"Creigh gave him a part-time job."

"No one told me."

Gino arched an eyebrow. "Didn't know anyone had to. Her shop after all." Gino tilted his head to the side. "What, you have a problem with that? Think she'll make a move on him or vice versa?"

Now that was funny. Creigh and Sergio. "Hell no. Her memory is longer than an elephant's. She can remember when he pissed in his bed. Not a sexy thing to know about a new potential lover."

"That's true." Gino laughed. "Serge isn't bringing the sexy; that's for sure. Besides, you should think of this in an entirely different way. He can keep an eye on her when he's at work."

"I won't have him spying on her." Creigh would hate it, and Dean would hate knowing what she did every hour of the day. Especially things that pleased her. It wasn't as if he didn't want her to be happy; he just didn't need the evidence of it rubbed in his face when it was more than obvious he wasn't content.

"Come on. It's me you're talking to." Gino held his hands out wide. "You don't have to pretend you're over her."

"I am over her. She's over me." A fact she couldn't have made more obvious if she tried. "We've both moved on. So drop it."

"*Move on*. Please. You don't know how to be without her. You've been chasing after her since she was Harlow's age. I sincerely doubt a little piece of paper is going to change all of that."

Frowning, Dean pulled his rag out of his back pocket and began to wipe his hands again, even though they weren't dirty. It was better than knocking his brother on his ass. "Don't say it like that. It sounds perverted." Just the thought of boys having the same sort of ideas for his daughter as he'd had for Creigh made Dean nauseated. Not his baby girl. Not ever.

"It's the truth."

"We were just kids back then."

"You might not have known about the birds and the bees, but you knew what you wanted, and it was Creigh. It's always been Creigh."

Dean grimaced. Gino wasn't telling Dean anything he didn't already know. He *was* the one living the life Gino was narrating, after all. "I went out with other girls, slept with other girls."

"Only because she didn't know you were alive. It took a long time for her to graduate from the tomboy stage, but when she did, that was it. You were a goner. Still are."

"If I'm such a goner, then why am I sitting here in my garage with you, instead of at my home cuddled up with her?"

"Because you fucked up."

"I fucked up?" Dean tossed the rag on the ground. "She's the one who filed for divorce, not me."

"No, but she didn't wake up one day and decide to leave you. Things were bad between the two of you for a while there. You know it and I know it."

"Oh and that's my fault?"

"I'm not saying it's anyone's fault."

"Then what are you saying?"

"You guys married too young. Had kids right away, then *bam*, you go from horny kids to adults. Things are bound to get screwed up when you move fast. Maybe she started to feel neglected and you began to wonder what you were missing out on. Other women started looking good to you."

"I was faithful." Every day of their life together up to the day she kicked him out. But even then he'd waited. Waited and hoped she would come back to her senses.

"Until you moved out."

"She kicked me out." What was with everyone rewriting history tonight?

"A fact you used as an excuse to fuck anything standing."

His brother couldn't have been any further from the truth if he tried. "The hell I did." Dean wasn't sure where Gino had gotten his information, but as usual it was all kinds of wrong. Yes, Dean had begun to date, but only when Creigh had made it more than clear he wasn't welcome back home. Some of those dates had led to more, but they were vastly outnumbered by the nights he spent sitting in his car outside his old house watching his family move on without him. "Whose side are you on, anyway?"

Instead of answering Dean's question, Gino plowed on. "You know what I don't understand?"

"The concept of bros before hos?" Dean grumbled before taking a deep drink from his beer.

"Is how," Gino continued as if his brother hadn't spoken, "you two have lasted apart this long. To be honest I never thought it would get as far as it did."

"Surprise, surprise; you don't know everything."

"It's apparently hereditary, little brother, because you don't either, and maybe it's time you admit it to yourself and to Creigh."

"She doesn't need me to admit anything." She didn't need him for anything. A fact she'd made more than apparent.

"Are you sure about that?"

"Yeah."

"Really?" The disbelief was evident in both his brother's voice and his leveled stare. "There's nothing you need to say to her? Nothing at all?"

Dean looked away. Okay, maybe there was something he needed to say after today's little altercation. Something he'd wanted to get off his chest and across to her before she'd darted out the door. "Well, maybe one thing."

"That's what I thought." Gino stretched and stood. "You know, I don't have plans for tonight."

"I'll alert the presses." His brother was the biggest himbo to ever walk the earth.

"And to save my niece and nephew from your shitty attitude, I'm going to hang out here while you go have a talk with Creigh."

Dean stared at his brother for a few seconds. If he went and did this, he'd never hear the end of it from Gino about how right he was, but at the same time, he'd get some face-to-face time alone with Creigh to do what it was he should have done earlier. It was a no-brainer. He was used to Gino giving him shit, but there was no way in hell Dean would ever allow himself to become used to the look of devastation in Creigh's eyes right before she'd left. The way he'd acted was wrong, and he had to make amends or risk losing what little feelings remained between them for good. "I'll be back in a couple of hours."

Chapter Two

Creigh was all cried out. She was tired, crampy, and hungry as hell, but she was way too pooped to do anything about it. It didn't help that nothing in her refrigerator was calling her name. It all looked bad. Even the watermelon she'd so desperately craved just two days ago had little appeal now.

Irritated, she closed the refrigerator with an extra thump and made her way back into the living room. Before she could take her seat, the doorbell rang, freezing her in midsquat. Groaning, she stood and glanced over at the clock on the DVD player. It was after eight. Even the Jesus slingers stopped coming around after nightfall.

The second she opened the door and peered out her security screen door, she let out a disgusted sigh. She was so not in the mood for this. Not at all. "What do you want?"

"I brought you a peace offering." Dean held up the plastic bag bearing the logo of her favorite deli sandwich shop. "Extra pepperoncini and sweet onion sauce. Pickles on the side."

Despite the hostility she so rightly felt toward him, Creigh was hungry, and she couldn't help but be pleased he was there. The bastard was good. "Pastrami?"

"Yes, you used to crave these around this point with both kids, so I figured..." He shrugged, as if his gesture would say what his lack of words couldn't.

"Thank you." She opened the door hesitantly and took the bag from him.

Instead of leaving as she'd hoped, Dean shoved his hands in his pockets and smiled. It had been so long since she'd seen him look at her in that matter, for a second Creigh just gawked at him. Good Lord, he was sexy. His smile did more for her than some erotic novels. How was it possible to want someone so much yet wish an anvil would fall out of the sky and land on his head at the same time?

"Creigh. Creigh."

It took a second for her brain to register he was speaking to her, but when it did, she felt like an idiot. Heat rose in her cheeks, and she mentally kicked her own ass. What was wrong with her lately? It seemed as if he couldn't be around without her body acting all wonky. "Yes?"

His smile faltered a bit. "Can I come in?"

The way he said it made her wonder if this wasn't the first time he'd asked. Either way, her answer was simple. "No. I'm in not in the mood to deal with—"

Dean held his hands up innocently. "No dealing. No arguing. I just want to apologize."

"Apologize? You... Well, hell." Creigh stepped back to allow him room to enter. "This I have to see. Where are the kids?"

"At my house. Gino is watching them for me."

She made sure she stepped back far enough so there would be no accidental touching when he entered the house, then waited until he was inside before closing the door behind him. "You know the drill." She handed him the sandwich bag, then turned and walked into the kitchen, where she took out silverware, plates, and mustard.

Creigh always had to have extra mustard. Some people were ranch dippers. Creigh was a mustard dipper. The yellow condiment just made the world a better place. After gathering her gear, she headed back into the living room and found Dean exactly where she thought she would, sitting Indian-style in front of the coffee table.

To his right he'd set up a little sitting area for her against the starburst orange couch by placing mounds of pillows, some lying flat on the floor and two others propped up against the foot of the couch, in a chairlike arrangement, obviously meant to be a seat for her on the floor.

Try as she might, she couldn't help but be touched by his consideration. Laughing, she shook her head and laid all her goodies out on the table. "I'm not that pregnant yet. But thank you."

"Favorite food and plush accommodations for your tush might all seem to be a bit of overkill, but it's laying the groundwork for one massive apology, so you might as well soak it up."

"Massive. Wow." Creigh made her way over to the makeshift chair and sat down, folding her hands primly on top of her tiny bulge. "This I have to see."

Dean separated the sandwiches, handing Creigh hers with all of her condiments included, then grabbed his and set it on the floor next to him, using his former ratty recliner as a backrest.

"So," she said, picking up her sub. "Let's hear it."

"You don't want to eat first? Arguments aren't good for the baby."

The words "like you care" bubbled to the surface, but she held them back. Dean didn't have to be gracious about this. It would nice if he was, but he didn't have to be, so she didn't want to push it. Besides, if the shoe were on the other foot, Creigh knew she would be less than thrilled her damn self. "I don't want to argue."

"But can we talk about this, without bloodshed? My blood, by the way."

"I hit you once." She smiled at the fond memory. "In the seventh grade, and you deserved it."

"I still say a bloody nose is in no way a fair and just retribution for snapping your bra strap. Admit it. You went too far."

She shrugged, deflecting his words as if they weren't anything more than the buzzing of a pesky fly. "You can still breathe out of it. Some would say I didn't go far enough."

"And I say those people can kiss my ass." Dean rubbed his nose as if he felt a phantom pain from the days of yore. "You have a hell of a right hook."

"Well, keep that in mind while you're here. Be nice or…" She raised her fist, letting her hand do the talking for her.

"Yes, ma'am."

Creigh drizzled the mustard on the sandwich before taking a bite. The spicy, meaty delight set her taste buds on fire. She loved it. "Mmm."

"I knew that would do the trick. I can already tell you're not eating enough."

Once again the urge to make a smart-ass remark about why he cared came fast and furious to her lips, but like before she refrained from acting out on it. They had enough animosity between them as it was. Besides, she was still waiting for the apology.

After placing the sandwich back on her plate, she picked up a napkin and wiped her mouth. Setting the napkin back down, she crossed her arms over her breasts and stared at Dean. "So…"

He held up his index finger. "First, let me say I was an ass."

Creigh liked the way this was going already. "Massive ass."

"Okay." His lips twitched. "A massive ass, but to be fair, you really hit me from out of left field today. I'm not sure if I could have, but I should have handled it better, and for that I apologize. To you"—his gaze shot down to her belly, then back to her face—"and to the little one you're carrying. If I recall correctly, they can hear things right about now."

She smiled despite herself. "I'll have to take your word on that." When she'd been pregnant with Harlow and Hamilton, Dean had become a fanatic for baby books. He had read *What to Expect When You're Expecting* and *What to Expect When Your Wife Is Expecting*.

"Do you forgive me, Creigh?" he asked, returning to his point.

The sincerity of his words made forgiving his earlier actions easy. Lord knew they had enough problems between them without adding this to the pile. Besides, this was the nicest he'd talked to her in months. As sad as it was, she was lapping it up. "Yes, I do."

"Good." Dean flashed her a quick smile before picking up his sub and then taking a big bite. Creigh couldn't help but notice his fingers and nails were embedded with oil and grime. Which only meant one thing.

"Working on the Impala again?" She glanced from his nail beds to his face with a little grin. "I must have really made you mad."

He frowned. "Why does everyone think the only time I work on the car is when I'm upset?"

"Because it is?" She fired back, amused at his inability to see himself clearly. "Who else is ragging on you?" But the second she asked, she knew the answer.

Tilting her head she regarded her ex and smiled. "Gino," she said at the same time Dean did.

"I knew it." She shook her head in amusement as she picked up her sandwich and took a bite. Her former brother-in-law was as bad as a fishwife. Nag, nag, nag. "So how's that going over there?" She asked with a mouthful of food, not worried at all about politeness. They'd been an open-bathroom kind of family. A little food in the teeth was nothing compared to the other things they'd witnessed over the years.

"I fucking hate it. He's driving me fucking insane. Stops by any ol' time he wants, with advice and beer, like he's the poor man's Dr. Phil. And if it's not him, it's my sister, with all her freaking kids, bringing casserole after casserole. I'm not sure who told Annabelle she could cook, but whoever it was lied."

"I knew moving over there was a bad idea," she teased.

"I assure you, it wasn't my first choice," he said sardonically around a mouthful of food. "I was quite happy where I was, miles and miles away from him."

Creigh's smile slid away. So much for the truce. After balling up her napkin, she set it down on the plate along with her half-eaten sandwich. As hungry as she'd been before, the idea of taking another bite right now made her sick to her stomach, and it had nothing to do with the baby.

"Well, thank you for stopping by with the food." She rose to her feet and stood over him, trying her best to keep her emotions at bay. "And for the apology. It really meant a lot."

He shot her a quick, confused look. "What did I say?"

"Nothing." She shook her head, not wanting to get into it.

"Don't lie. If I said something to make you mad, just let me know. I mean fuck." He dropped his sandwich onto his plate and rose, agitated. "Just say what's on your mind, Creigh."

"There's nothing on my mind." She looked away and placed her hand on her stomach. "I'm just done eating."

"Liar. We were having a semigood time." A frown line appeared between his dark brows. "Or as good as we've had in ages."

It was true. All true, and she was putting an end to it because she'd gotten her feelings hurt. But these were things she couldn't say to Dean. At best he wouldn't understand. At worst, he would mock her inability to take a joke. Either way she would be the loser in the whole mess, so she might as well call the evening to an end before it even progressed that far.

"Nothing to say. I see."

Creigh held her hands out palms up. "No. I'm fine. You apologized, which was very gracious of you, and you know, we're fine. Or fine-ish."

"If you're okay with everything, there's no need for me to rush off." His mouth set in a stubborn line. "It's not like we don't have things to talk about."

Moving to the couch, she sat down and curled her feet beneath her. "Okay. Let's talk about this. But like adults. The second you start in on me, the second I feel like you're putting me down or judging me, you're out of here. Pastrami sandwich or not. I'm not going to be talked down to in my own home. Is that clear?"

"Crystal." He sat down in front of her on the coffee table.

She braced herself for what was to come. "Then go on, talk."

Dean opened his mouth, then promptly closed it. There was a lot he wanted to say, but he was afraid it wasn't going to come out the way he intended, as usual. On the ride over, he'd thought long and hard about the conversation they'd had in the kitchen and everything he could have and should have done differently. He'd responded completely off the cuff, not giving himself enough time to process what she'd said before he spoke.

Even now, hours later, it was still hard for him to accept the fact she had not only slept with another man but was expecting a child. It wasn't just hard. It was painful, and downshifting from angry ex to responsible adult wasn't as easy. He was still raw from the divorce, but he was a bigger man than he'd been behaving lately, and it was about time he acted like it.

"First, let me say I was trying here"—he gestured around his former living room—"trying to be on my best behavior. I thought my asshole flag was flying pretty low, you know."

"No, you were fine." Her smile was as false as her words. "I told you, everything is fine. You didn't do anything."

Fine. Dean was really beginning to hate that word. "Then why the sudden change in demeanor? You went from joking around to wanting me gone."

"I just…" She hesitated for a second before continuing. "I don't know, really. What else is there to say? You apologized. I accepted. Let's just move on."

"We can't move on until we talk about"—his throat tightened, but he forced the words past his lips—"the baby."

A shadow crossed her face. "Haven't we talked about that part enough?"

"Not hardly. I'm assuming you're planning on telling the kids soon. You can't keep it a secret for much longer." Hell, he was surprised he hadn't figured it out before. Underneath the dark-circled eyes and her waning complexion, there were some very obvious side effects of the pregnancy already appearing. Her face was fuller, her hair seemed healthier, and her breasts were a bit larger. All telltale signs of the life growing inside her. "We need to tell them before they hear it from someone else."

"I know. I was thinking I'd tell them on Sunday when you brought them home."

Dean nodded. "Sounds wise. I think I should be here when you tell them." Creigh opened her mouth to object, but he continued. "This is going to be a shock to them, and we need to show a united front. Let them know nothing is going to change—except for the obvious—of course."

"You'd do that?" she asked, her voice husky but hopeful.

"Of course." He was a bit affronted she thought he wouldn't. Yes, things had completely sucked between them lately, the hostility more on his end than hers, but this was about family, about their kids, and he wouldn't leave her to face it alone.

"Then…thank you." She offered him a small smile, something he hadn't seen her do in a while. "I think that probably would be best."

"They're going to have questions." He would if he were them. "Lots of questions, and I think we should be prepared with our responses."

She nodded in agreement. "Okay."

"So let's start out with the obvious." He searched her eyes with his. "The father. Who is he?"

She stilled. "He is no one."

That was not what he wanted to hear. "I really hope that's not the answer you're going to give them. All that's going to do is rouse more questions."

"Who he is isn't important," Creigh said firmly. "He's not going to be in their lives or the baby's."

"And you're fine with that?"

She hesitated, and for a moment Dean thought she would concede, but then she lifted her chin, her resolve in place, stronger than ever. "I don't think Harlow or Hamilton are going to ask me that."

"I'm asking," he snapped, which of course was the wrong thing to do.

Creigh narrowed her gaze and dug in her heels. "Is this little Q and A for you or them?"

"Humor me," he said in a more calm and reasonable tone, trying to win her over with honey instead of vinegar.

"No."

God, she was stubborn as a bull. "Why the hell not? Are you still seeing him?"

"No."

"Were you seeing him long?"

A shadow passed over her face before she answered. "Not really."

"Did he force you? You can tell me." He tried to gentle his voice and keep his expression neutral even though he was seething on the inside. If this guy hurt her in any way, shape, or form, he was a dead man. No ifs, ands, or buts about it. "Did he?"

"No," she reassured him quickly. "It was nothing like that. I had sex with him willingly."

"Good." He let out a relieved sigh. "I'm glad that wasn't the case."

"I can't believe you thought it was."

"I was making sure. Men these days are crazy."

"Tell me about it." She stared at him pointedly.

Affronted, Dean jerked back. "I'm just looking out for you."

"You don't have to."

"It's a hard habit to break." Especially since he didn't want to.

"You're going to have to try."

He snorted. "It looks to me like you need looking after now more than ever."

Her eyes grew serious. "This baby isn't your responsibility, Dean. Neither am I."

"Then whose responsibility is it?"

"Mine." She pointed to herself.

That answer wasn't good enough. "You didn't get pregnant by yourself."

"And I didn't get pregnant with you, so don't worry. I can handle this."

"I know you can, but you shouldn't have to handle it alone. The father should man up and take on his share of the load."

"He doesn't want to, and I'm not going to force the issue. Besides, we're better off without him."

"He gave up his wants when he lay down with you," he reminded her, a bit irritated he had to.

"You're assuming we lay down."

The image her words drew forth made his blood boil. "If you're trying to piss me off, you're going about it the right way." He bit the inside of his cheek to stop himself from saying more. Being an asshole was a lot easier than being understanding, and it was chafing like hell not to fall back into old habits. After a few minutes of pained silenced, he spoke again. "What's his name?"

"None of your business."

"Is that hyphenated?"

A quick smiled flashed over Creigh's lips. "You're so stupid."

He took the insult in stride. At least he made her laugh, if only for a moment. "I just want to make sure he does right by you. If he wasn't ready to be a father, he shouldn't have engaged in the act that could make him one."

Creigh rolled her eyes. "Are you as prepared to marry every woman you sleep with on the off chance the condom breaks?"

"I didn't say you two should marry." The very idea turned his stomach. "But yes, I would be prepared to take care of my child if the situation was reversed."

"Well that's what makes you, *you*." She smiled faintly.

His mind was too clouded with the image of her with another man to appreciate the humor in her comment. All Dean could think of was the *how*. "So is that what happened?"

Creigh frowned. "Is what, what happened?"

"Did the condom break?"

Creigh picked up one of the accent pillows from the couch and buried her face in it. "Ugg...just stop," she muttered from behind the plush square.

"Tell me."

Annoyed, she slammed the pillow down onto her lap and looked up at him, chin raised defiantly. "You want to know all the details. Fine, here it is. We went to dinner, had drinks, then went back to his place and had sex in the missionary position. Which, including the time it took to undress, took fifteen to twenty minutes, after which he called me a cab, walked me to the door, and waited in the doorway as I did the walk of shame to the waiting car. The end. Happy?"

Dean's entire body was tense, his stomach sour. "Not at all."

"That makes two of us. Honestly, it would be comical if it wasn't so sad. Who gets pregnant the first time they have sex besides stupid teenagers and groupies?"

"You got pregnant on the first time with him?" he asked, testing the truth of her words.

"Yes. Funny, right? I'm like one of those NBC *The More You Know* commercials. Apparently when the condom companies say they're only ninety-seven percent effective, they're not kidding around."

Dean rubbed his hand over his eyes. He was having a hard time processing his emotions and an even harder time keeping his damn mouth shut. He wanted so badly to rage against her, yell at her, and punish her for being with another man, but he knew it would do him no good. Being pissed off and shouting wouldn't make her any less pregnant, and it wouldn't make him feel better, especially if he ended up alienating her in the process. He leaned his head back and stared at the ceiling, searching for divine grace.

"I'm so happy we're sharing; aren't you?"

Dean let out a rough chuckle and looked back at her. "Surprisingly, not so much."

"Yeah, imagine that. So is it your turn now?" She clasped her hands together and smiled mockingly at him. "You want to tell me about your latest conquest?"

"Do you want to hear?" he asked with all seriousness, because he would tell her if she did; then maybe they could start from scratch on equal footing once more.

She looked away, game forgotten. "No, bragging is so unbecoming."

"It's nothing to brag about it. Regardless of what you might think, I'm not out there sleeping around." Dean didn't know why he felt the need to explain, but he did.

Creigh looked back at him. "Have you slept with more than one person?"

"Yes." He hated the shimmer of pain that glimmered in her eyes, but he couldn't lie.

"Then you beat me," she said tersely.

Dean knew it wasn't his place to ask, but he found his lips forming the words nevertheless. "He was the only one?"

"Yes." She met his gaze head-on, leaving little doubt to the truth of her words. "And despite this conversation starting out as us being on the same page for the sake of the kids, I reserve the right not to tell them any of this."

"I can respect that." Besides, that little piece of information had been for him. "Speaking of the kids, I should probably get going." Dean stood and glanced down at his watch. "The last time I left them alone with Gino this long, he fleeced them for their allowance."

"I told them about playing poker with him. Your brother cheats."

"Trust me. I know." Dean walked over to the small mess he'd made and began to clean up.

"I can get that," she protested, rising to her feet. "It's not a big deal."

"For me either." He shoved his leftovers back in the bag they came in. "Besides, you need to rest. You look tired."

"Sweet talker."

"I always manage to put my foot in my mouth when I'm around you." Damn, he just couldn't win. Jerking his head toward the door, he gave a tired smile. "I'm going to go before I say anything else that might offend."

He turned and headed toward the door but stopped when he felt her hand on his arm. He glanced down at her hand before looking up at her in confusion.

"It's not *always*," she said softly before releasing her hold on him.

"Well, that's good to know." It wasn't much, but it was something.

Chapter Three

The sound of Harlow's bedroom door slamming rang out like a shot throughout the otherwise silent house. Creigh tried her best not to flinch and to keep her gaze away from Dean, who was leaning against the wall, watching her intently. Right now she needed to focus on Hamilton, whose eyes were as wide as saucers.

"You okay, Hambone?" She tried to keep her tone light.

He shrugged and looked down at his pants. He pulled at a loose thread on the olive and gray fatigues, all the while kicking his foot against the base of the couch. Normally Creigh would have chastised him for scuffing the love seat, but because of the situation at hand, she was willing to let it slide.

"Do you have any questions?" she asked, praying he did. Whys and hows were a lot better than silence in her book.

She moved from the recliner to his side and put her arm around his tiny little shoulders, worried about the added weight she was adding with her news. Sometimes, with all the pretend battles he fought to defend the world, she forgot how really young he was. Her little man was still just her little boy. "You know you can tell me anything. If you're upset about the baby, you can tell me. It's not like you have to be excited—right away," she added hopefully.

"I know." He cut his gaze to Dean for a quick second, then away.

What is that all about? Creigh looked to Dean for guidance. For someone who said he wanted to be there to show a united front, he'd been surprisingly silent throughout the whole exchange. Not that there was much he could add, but still, something would have been better than nothing.

Dean caught her gaze and gestured with his head for her to leave the room. Normally his high-handed suggestion would have grated on her nerves, but truthfully Creigh could think of little else to do. If Dean thought a man-to-man conversation could help, who was she to disagree?

Tired and weary to the bone, Creigh nodded her head, then focused her attention back on Hamilton. Leaning forward, she brushed her lips across his tightly coiled hair and breathed in his childlike scent. "I'm going to go lie down for a little bit before I start dinner. If you want to talk, you know where I am."

She left the room but didn't go far. Moving so she wouldn't be seen, she stood in the hallway and watched as Dean took her place beside Hamilton on the couch. Dean placed his arm around their son's shoulder and pulled him close, moving his head down so it was resting on top of Hamilton's. The stiffness so evident in their son only a few minutes earlier seemed to melt away as the two of them begin to speak in hushed tones.

Her heart ached at the sight. Even though she and Dean both tried their best to make the divorce as painless as possible for the kids, Creigh couldn't deny both children missed having Dean around full-time. It was a feeling she knew well.

Happy that Hamilton was at least talking to Dean, she turned around and left them to it. Before heading to her room, she stopped by Harlow's room and knocked gently on the door, opened it, and peered inside. As expected Harlow was lying on top of her purple princess duvet, her arms crossed over her chest and a petulant expression on her pretty brown face. Apparently the storming away hadn't helped her disposition much at all.

Even though Creigh knew it was going to take time, the rejection smarted nevertheless.

"I just wanted to let you know I was going to be in my room lying down if you wanted to talk." But from the look Harlow shot her, Creigh knew it was highly unlikely, especially when her daughter rolled over to face the wall, leaving Creigh to stare at her back. Ignoring the obvious dismissive gesture, Creigh put as much cheer in her voice and said, "I love you, baby." She didn't wait for a reply, closing the door and knowing instinctively there wouldn't be one.

Creigh's eyes burned from unshed tears, but she held it together until she was safely in her room. Once there, though, she gave into her pain and let the tears flow.

She closed the door firmly behind her, then made her way over to her bed, throwing herself down on the comforter much in the way she imagined her daughter had just minutes ago. Reverting back to her own childhood, she grabbed one edge of the quilt and rolled herself up in it burrito-style, so she was at the center of the warmth and comfort. Creigh was in desperate need of a hug, even if it was a manufactured one given by a comforter.

Her bedroom door opened some twenty minutes later. The noise of the creaking door alerted her from her cocoon and caused her to lift her head so she could see who it was. To her embarrassment, it was Dean, and he appeared highly amused to find her wrapped up in her comforter. Shutting the door behind him, he made his way over to the bed and bent his head to look into the center of the quilt. "There you are. For a second I thought the bed had swallowed you poltergeist-style."

"No, I'm fine." Mortified but fine. Creigh rolled out so she was lying flat and the covering was back in place on opposite sides of her. Taking a deep breath, she eased up and moved to the middle of the bed, where she crossed her legs. All the while she did this, Dean just stood back and watched with a shit-eating grin on his handsome face.

Great. Creigh undoubtedly had bed hair. Her eyes were bloodshot from crying, her nose stuffed, and what little makeup she had on earlier was either long gone or had seen better days. Either way, she wasn't about to win any beauty contest. And as usual, Dean was looking good. Tight jeans, clean gray T-shirt underneath an open long-sleeved black one. Basically his signature look that took him less than five minutes to perfect but always made her feel like she had to spend an extra hour dressing to look half as good as he did naturally.

Life was simply not fair. But that was a lesson everyone was learning today in her house. Irritated with the hand she'd been dealt, she snapped at the one person who could handle it. "Well, come on in. Don't bother to knock or anything." Even to her own ears, she sounded bitchy, but at this point it was either be a bitch or cry, and she was done crying in front of Dean.

Instead of firing back with an equally snappish reply, Dean had the good grace to look sheepish. "Sorry, force of habit." Dean took a few steps back toward the door. "Want me to go back out, then come back in?"

"No." Now she was just being stupid. "Please come in."

"Oh okay." He glanced around the room and frowned. "You redid the room." He pointed to the comforter. "That's new."

"Yes." Their old bedding held too many memories.

"It's nice," he said casually before changing the subject. "*So*, if it will make you feel better, I'd be more than happy to take her door off the hinge for slamming it. I was tempted to do it right then and there for being disrespectful, but figured it was best to let her stew in her own brattiness for a while longer. But enough time has gone by, and it won't take but a second to remove it. I promise you, if you leave the door off for a month, she won't ever slam it again. My folks taught Annabelle that lesson early on."

"Tempting, but I think I'll let her slide this time." Creigh shot him a soft, sad smile. "Harlow is taking a lot in right now. Did you notice when I first said it, she lit up like a Christmas tree, at least until she learned the father was an ex-boyfriend?"

In that brief second Harlow had been close to her dream, her parents getting back together. The disappointment that had filled Harlow's face would stay with Creigh forever. The only time she could remember seeing her daughter more upset was when she and Dean told them they were divorcing.

"I think she thought the baby was yours."

"You're going to have to give her some time. You've had four months to adjust to this. She's had an hour." Dean walked to her side and sat down on the edge of the bed. "Also you have to keep in mind Hamilton is the only prototype for her to base her younger sibling's images on. She's thinking Hamilton 2.0 is a bad thing. When she realizes this baby is no Hamilton, plus really cute and cuddly, she'll be over it in no time."

Creigh smiled faintly. "Can I get that in writing?"

"Absolutely." Dean's voice held conviction that soothed her. If anyone would know about sibling rivalry, it would be him.

"And Ham?" Was she going to have to wait on him too?

"We talked." Dean grinned. "He was a little confused about where babies came from."

Creigh frowned. "Then why didn't he say something to me?"

"It's a guy thing. There are some things you just don't want to talk about in front of your mom. Once I gave him the bare basics, he was all good. In fact, once that was out of the way, he seemed sort of excited about the idea of having a new sister."

"He did?" And she'd missed it.

"Apparently our son is very progressive. He says women are just as good soldiers as men are, and under his command he'll have her in fighting form in no time."

Creigh chuckled. Leave it to Hambone to make lemons into lemonade. "He really said that?"

"Sure did; then he went in search for one of his old camouflage shirts for the baby."

Her heart lightened for the first time since she discovered she was pregnant. It really was going to be all right. Smiling, she unconsciously placed her hand over her womb, giving the baby a bit of the good energy she was feeling. "Well, one out of two ain't bad for starters."

"Exactly." Dean's voice was wooden, but his gaze was intensely centered on her hand.

The brief moment of camaraderie seeped away, leaving Creigh feeling raw and exposed. Clearing her throat to garner his attention, she rose to her feet and offered him a weak smile. "Well, thank you for stopping by. I do appreciate it."

"It was nothing, and I'm in no big hurry to rush off. You can lay up here and rest, and I'll take care of dinner."

As ungrateful as it was, Creigh felt angered by his presumption. "Dean—"

"I've gotten real good at those tofu tacos Harlow likes; even Hambone is warming up to them. He calls them rations." Dean shrugged his shoulders. "But whatever works right."

"No, I don't think it's a good idea." And the reason she didn't was because it sounded too good. No, not just sounded, but felt too good. There was nothing she wanted more than to make today pajama day and climb in a fresh pair, then slip under the covers and not worry about if the kids were going to get dinner and a bath. Dean could do it all for her. He'd been the king of making sure she had plenty of time to rest, both when she was pregnant and when she wasn't.

He'd never been good at communicating, but he'd mastered the fine art of pampering to a tee. And as much as her body craved that sort of attention right now, her mind knew it was a bad, bad idea to become accustomed to having him around again just to watch him leave later on when things became too hot for him to handle.

"You craving something? You want me to run out and get sandwiches for you and the interloper?"

Interloper had been the same nickname he'd given Harlow and Hamilton when she'd been carrying them. The familiar phrase caused her throat to tighten. What she wouldn't give to go back in time and sleep with Dean instead. Not only would the sex have been better, it would have meant something, and it would be the two of them expecting this child. Not just her.

She was in this alone, and she needed to start acting like it. No more leaning on Dean. No more using him for hero support. She was going to have to learn how to lie in the bed she'd made.

"No," she said louder this time, with more force in her words. "Not just to the sandwiches but to the tacos and anything else you can magically make in five minutes or less. I'm saying no to you staying. You lent your support. Crisis adverted. You can go home now."

"I see," he said stiffly. "You want me to leave."

"I think it's...best."

"Best." He rose from the bed and stepped back. "For who?"

"For me," she said firmly, all the while thinking, for my heart.

"And it's always about you, isn't it, Creigh?" Her answer seemed to have infuriated him more. "Things got too hard in our marriage, and you wanted out, because working to fix it, well that made no damn sense at all."

"What does that have to do with anything?"

"Everything." He snorted and shook his head in disgust. "Let me ask you this. Are you sure this mystery father doesn't really want anything to do with the kid, or is it you who doesn't want him to? Because here I am, trying to help, and you can't give me the boot fast enough."

Is that what he thought? Is that what he really thought of her? Hurt, she stepped back and tried to distance herself from him emotionally and physically. "What I don't want is another fight, especially with you. This isn't your problem, Dean, and I don't know why you keep inserting yourself in it."

"Why are you so damned scared of needing me?" His dark, furious gaze never wavered from hers.

Creigh opened her mouth to fire off a snappy reply, then promptly shut it. She didn't have an answer for his question. Not one at all.

His jaw tightened. "That's what I thought." Dean walked to the door and pulled it open before striding through. She waited, expecting him to slam the door behind him, but instead he stood there for a brief moment. "I really wish I could figure out how to cut you out of my life as effectively as you've cut me out of yours. It really takes talent to be so cold."

Then he shut the door gently, his footsteps briskly moving away as Creigh sat back down on the bed in anger and dismay. Damn him and his platitudes. And damn her for her lies.

"Fuck it," Dean muttered under his breath as he made his way down the hall. He just couldn't win for losing with her. Nothing he did, nothing he said was ever right, and he was damned tired of trying. Goddamn it, when was he going to let her stop tying him in knots? He'd been right to keep his defenses up when she was around. She was fucking fatal. His own personal brand of kryptonite, and he was over it.

As upset as he was, Dean knew it was best he left as soon as possible. He didn't want to chance running into Creigh again. He didn't think he could handle being thrown out of his house three times in one lifetime. After calling out a quick good-bye to Hamilton, who was watching G.I. Joe on the couch, Dean made his way out the front door and down the steps.

Before he could make it to his car, however, the front door opened. "Dad."

The desperation in Harlow's voice stopped him in his tracks. Frowning, he turned and made his way over to the porch, where she was standing in the doorway. She looked so much like Creigh it was heartbreaking. He could remember back to the day she was born. He knew then she was going to break his heart one day. He never knew it was possible to love one person so much. "What's up, princess?"

Doubt clouded her hazel eyes. "Are you going home?"

Or to the first bar he ran across. "Yes. I have some stuff I need to do." Like get rip-roaring drunk.

"Can I come with you?"

Dean frowned. "You have school tomorrow, honey."

"I know." Harlow glanced behind her into the house for a second before coming outside completely. "I meant can I come home with you. To stay. I want to live with you."

He stared at her in amazement. Of all the things he'd expected her to say, asking to move in wasn't one of them. He stared at her in shock for a couple of seconds trying to figure out what to say. Of course he wanted her to live with him. He wanted them all to live together under the same roof. He missed the noise, the constant clutter, everything great and small. But jumping on this opportunity, when Creigh was down and Harlow was so upset, was just the wrong thing to do. "Princ—"

"I'd be a big help to you." She rushed forward, as if she could sense his response already. "I can do the laundry, vacuum, and help you keep the house nice and neat. And I'd be real good company for you." Her eyes watered with every word.

She was breaking his heart. "Harlow, come here." He pulled her the rest of the way to him and into his arms. Resting his chin on top of her soft golden hair, he sighed. Dean wished he had the words to make everything better for her, but he didn't. Nor could he give her what she wanted. "As much as I'd like to say yes, honey, I don't think it's a good idea."

"But—"

"No buts, honey." He pulled back so he could peer into her upturned face. "Your mom needs you right now, and as mad as you are, you need her too. You don't want to move out, and you and I both know it."

"She doesn't need me. She has Hamilton, and soon she'll have the new baby." Tears fell unchecked down her cheeks, the sight of them almost undoing him. Nothing could lay him low faster than his girls in pain. Which was part of his problem with Creigh. It wasn't in him to sit back and watch her struggle.

"And that's when she'll need you most. Babies are a lot of work, honey." Harlow made a disgusted faced that made him laugh. "But they're a lot of fun. You were too young to appreciate it with Hambone, but with this baby you'll be able to hold her and play with her. Doesn't that sound like fun?"

Harlow shrugged but didn't say anything.

"Do me a favor." Dean rubbed his hands up and down her arms. "Give it a try, and by the time the baby's been here for let's say six months, if you still feel the same, we'll talk about this again."

"You promise?"

"I promise," he said solemnly. Although he seriously doubted this would be an issue in a year. Harlow wasn't asking to move in with him because he was the better parent. She was asking him to strike out at Creigh, and as much as he wanted to take his ex-wife over his lap and punish her for the way things were going right now, he would never do anything to purposely hurt her. She was a good mother, a good person, and despite how angry he was with her right now, still the woman he loved and also the mother of his children. As long as he was living, his children would not disrespect her, no matter how upset they might be.

Lowering his voice, Dean spoke in a sterner voice. "Now I think you owe your mother an apology. Slamming the door was rude and almost earned you a first-class ticket to No-privacyville." He softened his tone a bit. "Where pesky little brothers run freely in your room at all hours of the day."

"*Dad!*" she protested, her face a mask of annoyance. Dean arched a brow but didn't say a word. After a few seconds, Harlow hunched her shoulders and looked away. "Fine. I'll apologize."

"Good. You should..." He glanced up and spotted Creigh standing in the doorway. For a second their gazes connected, but before he could say anything, she hurried past the door and out of sight. He wondered how long she'd been there, then mentally kicked himself for caring. He'd said what he said for Harlow's sake. Not Creigh's. Shaking his head, he cleared his mind and went back to the conversation at hand. "Think of something nice you can do for your mom. This is not in lieu of apologizing, by the way. You still have to do that. *Capisci?*"

"Capisci." A small smile formed on her heart-shaped lips. "I love you, Dad." Harlow slipped her arms around his neck and squeezed tight.

As always, Dean's throat got a little tight when she said that. "I love you too, princess. Now scat." He released her, then landed a playful swat on her behind as she headed back inside.

Dean watched until she entered the house and shut the door before he turned and headed to his truck. He knew she would do as promised and apologize to her mother, even though it wasn't what she wanted to do. Harlow was a good girl, even if she did have his temperament. Besides, they were all learning to do things they didn't want to these days. Sighing heavily and wondering just how things had gotten so far, Dean opened the door to his truck and climbed in. His earlier thoughts about visiting a bar seemed like an even better idea now, and he knew just the one to go to.

* * *

The sound of the baseball game playing on the flat-screen greeted Dean the second he opened the door to his brother's bar. Hooters this place wasn't, although Gino's hot-wings recipe had greatly improved. De Luca's Tavern was, at best, a man cave. An old-fashioned watering hole with cable. The beer was cold, the burgers greasy, and there was always a game on. It was Gino's idea of heaven and of late had become Dean's second home.

He didn't go there to drink, though. He could do that in his living room while wearing nothing but his underwear. Dean went for the noise. It was hard to feel lonely in a room full of drunks. Dean nodded his head to the regulars he recognized as he made his way over to the bar.

To his delight, it wasn't just his eldest brother he found, but his youngest there as well. The two men were working the busy bar, filling beer mugs and taking orders. Even from a distance the resemblance between the brothers was extremely noticeable, not helped at all by the matching black T-shirts they wore with the bar's logo on it. Gino had a good ten years on Sergio and had been looking after him ever since their parents died seven years ago. At the time Gino was a construction worker with a small place of his own, doing a bunch of nothing. He instantly moved in to their parents' house and took over. But just because Gino had been granted custody over their younger brother, it didn't mean he'd been the only one taking care of him.

Everyone had pitched in—neighbors, cousins, aunts, and uncles, proving the old adage that it did indeed take a village. Now his little brother was a few inches taller than them both and working part-time at the bar, the flower shop with Creigh, and going to school.

Every time Dean looked at Sergio, he knew his parents would be proud of all of them and how they all turned out. Even if they wouldn't have been pleased with the divorce. His parents were very old-fashioned, and a lot of his ways and beliefs came from the foundation his father had laid out for him.

Smiling and feeling more relaxed than he had all weekend, Dean made his way over to the bar and sat down across from his brother on an empty stool. The younger man grinned when he saw Dean.

"Beer me, little brother."

"Sure thing, big brother." Sergio stepped away to fill the order. While he was doing that, Dean took in the view. The new pool table Gino had installed seemed like it was a crowd-pleaser. It fit just fine in the back next to the jukebox and dartboard.

"Here you go." Sergio popped the top before handing it to Dean, then opened two more, slipping one to Gino, who came up alongside them.

"Taking care of a bill." Gino grabbed the beer on his way by. "Be right back."

"Busy night?" Dean asked.

"Little bit. College kids mostly." Sergio gestured with his head to the perky sorority-type chicks down at the end of the bar. "Tips were good."

Dean wasn't surprised. His brother was a handsome man. They all were, but he sometimes wondered if God used him and Gino as the practice runs before blessing their parents with Sergio. Dean considered it a godsend they never had to compete for the same girl growing up, because even though the men looked very similar to one another, there was something just a bit more about Sergio that would have made it an unfair fight. Added on top of the fact his brother was generally a good guy, it was downright sickening.

"I'm back and thirstier than fuck." Gino slapped a white towel over his shoulder, then held his beer up and grinned. "It's toasting time."

"Ugg." Dean rolled his eyes at the cornball tradition to see who would get the next beer free. "Not this old thing."

"Yes, this old thing. Best line wins. I'll start it. It's a classic, boys. Join in if you know it. 'Here's to the bee that stung the bull and started the bull to bucking.'"

Dean smiled, for he did know it.

"'And here's to Adam, who stuck it to Eve,'" Dean and Sergio joined in, "'and started the world to fucking.'"

The three men raised their bottles in the air, then each took a drink simultaneously.

"Hear, hear," Dean said, as Gino bowed regally.

"My turn." Sergio jiggled his bottle to garner their attention. "I'm ready. 'Here's to hell. May my stay there be as much fun as my way there.'"

"Excellent, little brother." Dean laughed before chugging down another gulp of beer.

"You ready?" Gino asked.

There was no time like the present to share his good news. "Yes. I'd like to make a toast my brothers." Each man raised his bottle once more. "To Creigh and her new baby. May they live long and prosper." Dean took a deep drink, but he was the only one. His brothers still had their hands raised, but their mouths were open wide in shock. "What? Was that too *Star Trek*ish?"

Gino was the first to recover, lowering his bottle back to the bar. "That didn't rhyme. Nor was it the slightest bit funny."

"I thought the same thing when she told me on Friday."

"Fuck." Gino's eyes widened. "I didn't know you two were…"

"We aren't."

"Oh." Gino went and grabbed another bottle of beer and slammed it down in front of Dean. "You win. Hands down."

"I'm feeling really out of the loop right now. When did this happen?" Sergio asked with a frown.

"Apparently four months ago." Dean toyed with the label of the bottle he was still drinking.

"But…I've been working at her shop on the weekends for like a month. I haven't noticed at all."

Dean shrugged. He'd seen her twice a week for four months and hadn't noticed either. "She's showing, but not too much."

"So," Gino interrupted loudly. "Is this the part where you say the father is…"

"Unknown to me." A fact that was still rubbing him raw.

"Well then, there's only one thing to do," Gino said out of the blue.

"Close the bar and grab the bats," Sergio offered.

Dean smiled. Now that was a brother.

"No. Fuck him. Fuck her." Gino frowned. "It's time to get you laid."

"I could have sworn just yesterday you were putting the entire problem with our relationship on my shoulders, and you were hinting—strongly, I might add—you thought she and I should get back together."

"Clearly I was wrong."

"Or were you?" Sergio chimed in. "The guy's a no-show, right?"

"Right." Dean nodded.

Sergio continued. "You still have feelings for her, right?"

Try as he might not to, he did. And they just weren't going away. "Right."

"Then all you have to do is go in there and save the day." Sergio smiled widely. "Right?"

"Wrong." Gino frowned and shook his head. "She dumped you, man. She no longer has feelings for you."

Dean shook his head. "I don't believe that. Yes, she dumped me, but I think she still cares."

"That's the alcohol talking," Gino protested.

Dean laughed. "I haven't even finished my first beer."

"Then that's the alcohol *not* talking. Have another drink." Gino pushed the bottle closer to him. "Maybe you'll wise up."

"Or maybe I won't. You said it yourself. I've been chasing her so long, I don't know how not to."

"She's pregnant with someone else's kid," Gino said as if Dean needed the reminder.

"Yes. Yes, she is." That was the one fact he could not dispute. But for the first time, hearing it out loud wasn't quite so painful. It was almost normal. Creigh was having a baby, and saying it over and over didn't make the world implode or his head explode. It was just a baby. And if Hambone was planning to mold her into a soldier, why couldn't Dean just mold her into another daughter? Where she came from wouldn't matter so much once she was here. She'd love the man who raised her. DNA be damned.

Gino's eyes narrowed. "I do not like that look on your face."

"Well, that sucks for you," Dean teased, feeling a bit better than he had before. There were still so many things wrong with his and Creigh's relationship, but suddenly he realized this baby didn't have to be one.

Gino tossed a handful of pretzels at Dean. "Whatever you're thinking, stop it. You need a vacation. From your life and from your ex-wife."

"No, what I need is to get her back." The minute he said it, he realized it was the truth.

Gino leaned forward and rapped his knuckles on Dean's skull. "Hello. Anyone in there? She doesn't want you back."

Dean pulled back and batted his brother's hand away. "You don't know that." Dean could be as stubborn as the next De Luca.

But his obstinacy didn't slow Gino down. "The divorce courts do. She left you. Broke your heart, man."

"Which means she's the only one who can ever fix it," Sergio interjected.

The other two men stopped talking and turned their attention to their younger brother, who suddenly didn't seem so little anymore. Even though Sergio was way over six feet tall now, tunnel vision wouldn't allow either Dean or Gino to see him as anything other than the younger, smaller, weaker kid brother. Well, at least till now. Dean was staring at Sergio in a whole new light. The kid was actually making sense. Sounded as if there was a chance he'd actually gotten his tip wet a time or two.

Gino, on the other hand, didn't appear to be having an epiphany at all. "What do you know?"

Gino's hypocrisy made Dean burst out laughing. "Aren't you the same person who told me I shouldn't discount squirt here just because he's learning to wipe his own ass?"

"Since when have you ever listened to me?"

Dean smiled. "Exactly." Rising from his seat, he reached in his back pocket and pulled out his wallet, then tossed a few bills down on the bar to cover his tab.

"No, take this back." Gino grabbed the money and handed it back to him. "You're going to need it for therapy."

Sergio snatched the bills out of Gino's hand and it handed it to Dean. "Or flowers. A good place to start."

Gino groaned and pulled the white towel off his shoulder and snapped it at his baby brother. "You're not helping."

"No, I think he is." Dean gladly took back the money Sergio gave him and reached over the bar to slap his brother on his arm in camaraderie. "You grew up on me, man."

Sergio shrugged. "It was bound to happen."

"So I see." Dean squeezed Sergio's shoulder. "I'll see you guys later."

"Don't do anything stupid," Gino yelled after him.

To which Dean had no reply. Trying to hook up with his ex-wife who was pregnant by another man was more than stupid. It was insane.

Chapter Four

Creigh arrived at work the next morning determined to put the weekend out her mind. It was a new day, and she was going to focus on the positives and not the negatives, even if it killed her. She parked her car in its usual spot and made her way into the flower shop she co-owned with her paternal cousin, A-mei Gibbs.

A-mei had already opened the store three hours earlier and was now sitting behind the counter with her head buried in a book. The only visible part of her caramel brown skin was her forehead, but even that was slightly covered by a few strands of her jet-black hair. The rest of her thick hair was twisted in a knot on top of her head and held up with her customary chopsticks, a nod to her mother's heritage.

When the bell over the door went off, signaling Creigh's arrival, A-mei looked up and smiled. "Hey, lady."

"Hey," she called back. The mingling floral scents filled her nose as she passed by the artfully arranged bouquets and arrangements and made her way to the counter. The constant reminder of spring was one of the best things about being a florist.

"How was your day off?" A-mei asked as Creigh neared.

"I've seen fire and I've seen rain," she teased as she walked behind the counter and set her purse underneath the register.

"That doesn't sound good." Concern filled A-mei's dark brown almond-shaped eyes. "Weekend from hell?"

"You could say that. I told the kids and Dean about the baby."

"Oh." A-mei set the paperback novel she'd been reading spine-up on the counter. "How did that go?"

"Bad, then surprisingly good." Creigh smiled ruefully. "Then bad again."

Sighing, A-mei hopped off the stool and pulled her short jean skirt down. The action didn't help much. A-mei had killer legs and an affinity for showing them off. Actually, there wasn't much of her body that wasn't killer or didn't have an outfit that complemented it. Her cousin was a clotheshorse who enjoyed all things pretty and feminine. "Tell me what happened."

Creigh wasted no time in bringing her cousin up to date on everything that had occurred on Friday and Sunday.

"So let me get this straight. He offered to cook dinner so you could rest?"

"Yes."

A-mei slapped her hand down on the table. "That bastard. I hate it when a guy offers to do something nice for me, especially after I break up with him. How dare he?"

When A-mei said it like that, Creigh felt a little stupid. Apparently she'd told the story wrong, or else her cousin would be squarely on her side. "Okay, you're missing the point here."

"Which would be…" A-mei let her words trail off.

"He's doing it again."

"What exactly would *it* be?"

"Bulldozing his way over me."

A-mei stared at her blankly. "By offering to cook you dinner?"

"It would start at dinner; then maybe next week he'd come over to cut the front lawn or change a tire or put together a crib. I know Dean. This would snowball back into me being too dependent on him. You know how it was before."

"And I know what it was like after. I have to tell you, I think *after* is worse than *before*. You're miserable. You miss him, and despite the time apart, you still love him."

A-mei was absolutely right. Creigh was still in love with Dean. That's why she had to push him away. Yes, his bulldozing was a bit annoying, but it was more touching than anything else. As usual, when the chips were down, Dean came to the rescue on his white steed to save the day.

Because of the type of man Dean was, Creigh knew he would automatically do what he thought was the right thing, which in this case she could already see what that meant. Step in and do the job the baby's father wouldn't. Although she would love to have his strong shoulder to lean on again, she knew it wasn't fair to him. She cared too much about him to do that to him. "What do you want me to say?" she asked after a few seconds. "That I messed up? That I should have never asked for the divorce?"

"If it's the truth."

"I am n—"

The bell over the door went off again, which caused both women to immediately quiet and face the door. Creigh pasted a fake smile on her face, but that quickly melted into a sincere one when she recognized the face of her former brother-in-law and part-time employee, Sergio.

The tall, good-looking young man walked to the front of the counter with a smile on his handsome face. "Ladies," he said, placing his motorcycle helmet on the counter. "How's it going?"

"Good," A-mei said, her voice filling with pleasure.

It was a sentiment Creigh understood. Out of all of Dean's siblings, Sergio was her favorite. He'd been such a good kid, following behind them wherever they went. There were great spaces of time when Creigh forgot he was Dean's brother and not her own. Her familial concern turned into maternal concern when his parents passed. Even now, she couldn't help but want to cuddle him and treat him like the ten-year-old boy he once was. "Sergio. What are you doing here? Shouldn't you be in school?"

He rolled his eyes. "Just here to pick up my check, *Mom*. Bedsides, it's not prison. We are allowed time off for good behavior."

"Smart-ass." She popped open the register and picked up the drawer. She shuffled through the checks to get to the white envelope bearing his name. After picking it up and placing the drawer back on top, she closed the register and handed the check over to Sergio. "Don't spend it all in one place."

"He's not a kid, Creigh, and it's not an allowance," A-mei said in a dry tone. "I'm sure the candy stores are safe."

Creigh shot her cousin a curious stare, not that the other woman noticed. She was too busy staring at Sergio. "I know he's not a kid," Creigh said.

It would be hard not to recognize that. Sergio might be younger than they were, but as handsome and muscular as he was, she would have to be a nostalgic fool to think he was a child.

"What are you doing for the rest of the day?" A-mei asked out of the blue.

"Bank, back to school, candy store," he said, tossing a quick wink Creigh's way. "Then home to study."

"Sounds…fun," A-mei said sarcastically.

He grinned. "Tell me about it."

"Are you studying for a big test tonight?" A-mei asked, her voice casual and unassuming.

"No, just hitting the books in general."

"Oh, then are you in the mood to make a little extra money? We have a delivery coming this evening, and I can use the extra help."

Creigh frowned and looked at her cousin. "You didn't tell me we had a delivery. I can stay and help."

"I didn't tell you for a reason. I don't want your help. The bags of fertilizer are heavy and filled with stuff you don't need to be breathing in."

"And you don't want to be lifting in your condition."

A-mei and Creigh turned in unison to look Sergio. "What condition?" Creigh asked, startled.

"Mum…" Sergio's gaze instantly dropped to her stomach before rising to meet her gaze once more. "No condition." He backpedaled unsuccessfully.

"You know."

"Know what?" He tried for innocence and fell flat.

"He knows." A-mei laughed.

Creigh narrowed her gaze. "How do you know?"

"Can we just pretend like none of this happened?"

"Nope." Oh no, he wasn't getting off that easily. "We can't."

"It's not a big deal," he protested. "I'm sure if he knew it was a secret, he wouldn't have said anything."

Creigh's jaw tightened. "Right. What else did he say?"

"Oh, I don't think so. You are not putting me in the middle of this."

"Too late, buddy. You're all ready in the mid—" Before she could continue, her cell phone rang. Taking it out of her sweater pocket, she glanced down at the number. When she recognized the phone number for Harlow's school, she held up her index finger and said, "Hold that thought. I'm not done with you."

Walking a few feet away, she answered her cell. "Hello."

"Mom." Harlow's voice sounded frantic and choppy, as if she was close to tears.

"What's wrong?" Every muscle in Creigh's body stiffened in preparation for bad news.

"My science report is due today, and I can't find it anywhere. I put it my backpack; I know I did, but I can't find it anywhere."

Creigh let out a breath she hadn't realized she'd been holding and said a little silent prayer of thanks before speaking. "When was the last time you worked on it?"

"I worked on it at Dad's, but I cleaned up my folder last night at home, and I know it was in there."

"Are you absolutely sure?"

Her daughter hesitated. "No. Can you check for me? It's very important. It's worth forty percent of my grade. Mr. Lorne said if I turn it in by the end of the day, he'll still give me full credit. Please, Mommy."

Oh now she was *Mommy*. "I'll go look. Call me after your next class."

"I will. Thanks, Mom. You're the best."

"Uh-huh," she said drily. "Tell me something I don't know."

"Oh, Mom. Can you call Dad and ask him to check his house too?"

"Har—"

A loud ringing in the background blared over the line. "That was the bell. I have to go. Thanks a million."

Before Creigh could respond, her daughter disconnected, leaving Creigh cursing under her breath. One day. One day without drama was all she asked for.

"Everything okay?" A-mei asked from behind her.

"Just peachy." Creigh took a deep calming breath before turning back. "Think you can hold the fort down for a bit longer? I have to go on recon duty."

"Of course."

"Wonderful. I owe you one. And you." Creigh focused her attention on Sergio. "Don't think you're getting off so easy. You and I are going to have a conversation."

"Can't wait."

Neither could she.

* * *

The ringing doorbell stirred Dean from a light slumber. Blinking, he glanced around his living room, trying to gather his bearings. Smacking his lips, he sat up and ran his hand through his hair, shaking off the lingering fog from his head.

God, he was tired.

The doorbell rang again, this time followed by a heavy pounding. Irritated at the commotion, he rose from the couch and made his way over to the entrance, intent on giving whoever was on the other side a piece of his mind. Unlocking the door, he swung it open, words on the ready.

They quickly died in his throat when he realized it was Creigh on the other side.

"What's going on?" Dean opened the door so she could pass, still a bit groggy from the nap.

"I should be asking you." Creigh brushed past him and into the living room. Her expression was far from that of someone who was pleased. This time Dean knew he was in the clear. All he'd been doing was lying on the couch like putty. "I've been trying to call you for the last forty minutes. I was beginning to think something was wrong with you." Creigh turned on him and held out her hand. Her index finger and her thumb were just inches apart. "I was this close to calling your brother and the cops. And in that order."

Dean cringed as he closed the door and made his way over to the couch, giving her the recliner because he knew it was much easier for her to get up out of it. Sitting down, he cast a quick guilty glance at the house phone, which was lying on the floor, half under the table. He'd taken it off the hook in his bid for peace and quiet. He hadn't even bothered turning his cell on, and now he was paying for it, rightfully so. Anything could have happened to the kids, might have still, for all he knew.

Manning up, he took the responsibility and the blame. "Sorry, that was irresponsible of me. I was taking a sick day, and those fools at the plant kept calling me. I got tired of it and turned the phones off."

The angry look on her face quickly morphed into one of concern. "Are you okay?"

The instant melt touched him. She cared, even though he knew she didn't want to. "I was having a little vision problem."

"Oh no." Creigh leaned in closer to him and peered intently into his eyes, as if her supermom powers could see right through his corneas and to the issue at hand. "What's wrong?"

"I couldn't see myself going to work today."

"Oh." She let out a relieved sigh. "I was worried there for a moment."

Dean quirked a brow. "Oh really?"

"Well, you know." She glanced away as if embarrassed by her obvious concern and pushed a strand of her silky dark brunette hair behind her ear. She was looking exceptionally lovely today. The pretty orange peasant shirt she wore complemented her dark brown skin and brought to mind, for some random reason, the sun setting on the Caribbean. It also billowed a little in the front, in what he could only surmise was an attempt to keep the pregnancy under wraps for a bit longer. Either way, she looked beautiful, and it would be very un-Italian of him to see a beautiful woman and not compliment her. He might even get kicked out of NIAF for it.

"I like that shirt on you." He reached out and fingered the soft material. "And I like that you care enough to worry."

"Some habits are harder to break than others."

He toyed with the material, loving the feel of it, loving even more that it was the only thing standing between him and Creigh's milky brown skin. "I've been saying that for a while."

"If I didn't know better, I'd say you faked sickness just to win the argument to see if you'd get a reaction from me."

She pulled her shirt free of him, but not in a mean-spirited or irritable manner. If Dean didn't know better, he would say that his little wildcat was feeling a bit shy.

"You came to my house, *cara*." He added his pet name for her softly, smiling on the inside when she blushed. Creigh had always loved it when he spoke Italian to her, especially when he did it when they were in bed.

"Your house." She shook her head as if to clear her thoughts and stood up. "I forgot I'm here for a reason."

"Pity the reason's not me."

Creigh started at his comment but then forged on. "Harlow can't find her science report."

Dean frowned. "The one that was due today?"

His knowledge appeared to floor Creigh. "You knew about that?"

Dean might have fallen down on the job as a husband, but he was most proud of his interaction and his participation with his children. With them, he was never second-rate. "Didn't you?"

"Yes, I just..." She waved her hand as if shooing the conversation away. "Never mind. Have you seen it? I've looked everywhere at home, and I can't find it."

"I haven't seen anything, but of course I wasn't looking for a report either." He waved his hand around his living room, which was still showing signs of the kids' last visit.

"Why don't you check down here, and I'll go search her room. It's bound to turn up somewhere."

"Okay."

Dean took the stairs two at time in an attempt to find the paper in a hurry. Harlow took her schoolwork a little more seriously than he would prefer. He worried she would get an ulcer if she wasn't careful. The worst part was, it was all pressure she put on herself to be the best. He and Creigh were really going to have to work on a way to get that under control. And soon. After searching not only Harlow's, but Hamilton's and his own room as well, Dean made his way back downstairs to deliver the bad news to Creigh. To his surprise, though, Creigh wasn't in the living room where he'd left her. He softly called out her name as he turned the hall and headed into the kitchen. When he neared the doorway, he spotted her shuffling through papers on the small round table in the corner.

"No luck."

"Me either." Her voice was wooden, her shoulders stiff, her demeanor completely different than it was just minutes ago.

Great. What did he do now? "What's wrong?"

"What happened to the wall?" She spoke without looking up at the spot in question, her gaze still focused on the pile in front of her.

Dean groaned and rubbed his hand over his eyes. Just what he needed, more proof of his incompetence. He was batting a thousand today. "The wall ran into my fist."

"Funny, I didn't notice that Friday."

"Yeah," he admitted. "Probably happened after you left." Like two minutes after.

"Probably?"

He hadn't imagined he could possibly feel worse than he did when he let loose and put his hand through the wall. Man, was he wrong. "It's not a big deal."

"You assaulted your home. I would disagree."

"Creigh." He sighed. "I…" Dean tried to think of something to say that could explain his testosterone-laden actions, but nothing came to mind. "It's not a big deal."

"Uh-huh." She sounded less than convinced.

Dean let out a frustrated breath. "Will you look at me?" he asked, tired of staring at the top of her head.

She glanced up, and he realized why she hadn't before. Her big brown eyes were shimmering with unshed tears.

To his dismay, a few wayward drops escaped, breaking his heart as they trailed down her face. "Cara." He walked over to her side but stopped short of touching her. They were on such fragile ground as it was, two steps forward, two giant leaps back, and he was getting damn tired of the moving around. "Don't upset yourself."

She swiped angrily at her cheek. "Stupid pregnancy hormones. Just ignore me. It's nothing."

"It's not nothing." His arms itched to wrap around her.

"Yes, it is. I feel so stupid."

"I assure you not half as stupid as I felt trying to explain to Hamilton why I punched the wall. He was so impressed with my show of strength he begged me not to fix it right away." Dean walked over to the wall and pointed to a small smudge beneath the hole he made. "See this? He tried to copy me. Didn't quite make it, which strangely made my excellent example of fatherhood even more impressive to him."

"That sounds like him." She laughed softly. After wiping her face dry, she took a deep breath; then she shot him a smile that didn't quite reach her eyes. "Okay, hormonal break over. Back to work." Creigh started to shuffle through the papers on the table once more as if nothing out of the ordinary had just occurred. "If you want, you can just wait in the other room. I'll be done in a second and out of your hair."

Irritated, Dean watched her pull away. Creigh was distancing herself from him just the way she had a year ago, right before she'd asked for the divorce. He hadn't understood what it meant then, but he damn sure knew what it meant now, and he wasn't going to sit idly by this time and watch it happen. "You sure you don't have that the other way around?"

She glanced up and frowned. "What do you mean?"

"It seems like I'm the one bothering you."

"Well, you weren't until you just said that." Creigh pushed the papers to the side, fanning them out on the table. "I don't see it. She must have saved it on the computer. I'll go see if I can retrieve it from there. Sorry for the interruption."

"Not half as sorry as I am." Because all she did was remind him of what he no longer had.

Creigh's head snapped back as if she'd been hit. "Trust me, I didn't want to come over here any more than you wanted me to."

"Creigh, I sincerely doubt you have a clue about what I want." Shaking her head, she went to move past him to leave, but Dean grabbed hold of her arm and spun her around until she was facing him. "But I'd be more than happy to show you."

Desperate to get a reaction from her that wasn't cool indifference, Dean lowered his mouth over hers and kissed her.

Chapter Five

Despite herself, Creigh groaned as Dean swept his tongue boldly into her mouth, his lips demanding and unyielding. The familiar taste of him rocked her to her core. She didn't want to enjoy the sensations, but her body betrayed her. Wrapping her arms around his neck, she pressed herself close to him.

Without breaking the kiss, he lifted her in his strong arms and sat her down on the cluttered table. Creigh automatically opened her legs and pulled her skirt up frantically to make room for Dean to step between her splayed thighs. He wasted no time doing so, pressing his rapidly growing erection against the apex of her sex, all the while continuing to drive her to distraction with his tongue.

Her heart raced from the contact of his hard, lean body and from the taste of his sweet lips. It had been so long since she'd felt his touch, she didn't know how to act. In the past, she would have just jumped on him ninja-monkey-style, pushed him to the floor, and taken what she needed from him. But now the situation was so out of the ordinary it bordered on ridiculous. They were divorced, she was pregnant with some other man's baby, and yet here she was, kissing him with all the passion she held inside her. If there was a level of hell filled with slutty women who made stupid mistakes, she would be their queen. But hell was hopefully eons away, so she wasn't going to worry about it now. Instead she was going to live in the present and question her sanity later.

Just when she thought she couldn't take another second of his soul-searing kiss, Dean entangled his hand in her hair and pulled her head back so she was staring directly into his intense hazel eyes. "You're putting on this big act, Creigh. This little 'Miss Independent, I don't need anybody' act, but it doesn't flow with me."

"I..." She reached her hand up behind her, grabbed his wrist, and tried to free herself from his overpowering hold. "It's not an act. I don't need..."

Dean leaned forward and nipped at her lips. One nip for every word. "You." Nip. "Need." Nip. "Me." He laved her plump bottom lip with his tongue before continuing once more. "Because I remember what you were like with the other kids. How you'd get moody at the drop of the hat. Crying one second, railing against me another," he said in a husky voice. "But I also remember we found the best cure for your hormonal madness. All it took was a few long, hard strokes from my cock, and you were right as rain once more."

As much as Creigh would have loved to deny his words and throw them back in his face, she couldn't. Dean was so right. Creigh had to have been the strangest pregnant person in the universe, because when she'd been carrying her oldest two, all she'd craved was sex. Some women wanted ice cream. She even had a friend who secretly craved dirt.

Creigh wanted cock. Lots and lots of cock. And this time was no exception.

She felt aroused all the time. There wasn't a night that had gone by she hadn't pleasured herself once or twice in a row just to be able to sleep. Her hormones were off the chart, so much so that during her first pregnancy, she'd talked to her doctor about the spike in her sex drive. The bastard had the nerve to smile and tell Dean just to enjoy it, because it wouldn't last long. Three pregnancies seemed like an awful long time to her.

"I've learned to adapt to singlehood. I can be right as rain in three minutes or less now, with half the mess."

His grip tightened in her hair. "And half the pleasure, I'm sure."

"You're wrong."

"Really? Let's find out." Acting swiftly, he pushed her free-flowing peasant shirt down her shoulders and past her breasts, leaving the material bunched up above her elbows, effectively limiting just how much arm movement she would have. From the evil grin he sent her when she tested the bonds of the shirt, he knew exactly what he'd done.

Once she was bound, Dean turned his attention to her breasts. With a predatory look in his eyes, he cupped her heavy mounds, running his thumbs over her nipples poking up underneath the lacy fabric of her plum-colored bra. The wired bra molded her large breasts just right, lifting her tender flesh high like a sacrificial offering.

"Dean. This is a bad idea." The tightness of her throat made her halfhearted protest sound even weaker. "We...we shouldn't—"

"The hell we shouldn't." His features were taut, his expression hot with desire. "Come, cara. Tell me how I compare to your Duracell-powered lover." Dean pulled her bra straps halfway down her arms, then freed her breasts from their lacy confines. He nudged her back a bit, forcing her to use her hands to hold herself up. The new position made her breasts jut out vulgarly like a bow on a ship and caused Dean to growl in appreciation.

Her nipples tightened under his stare, so responsive, so aroused yet so tender. But no matter how sensitive her breasts were, Creigh always enjoyed having them played with, sometimes intensely and for long amounts of time. Lucky for her, Dean was a breast man and loved nothing more than to spend hours with his lips surrounding her nipples.

"God, I'd forgotten how perfect you are." Leaning forward, he took her right nipple between his lips and suckled hard.

Gasping, Creigh dropped her head, arched her back, and pushed her breasts up to him. He responded to her obvious pleasure by increasing the pressure with his mouth while using his fingers to twist and toy with the other. He teased and tormented her for a good ten minutes, making sure he gave both breasts the exact amount of pleasure-pain he knew she loved so much.

Once he was done driving her to distraction, he released her nipples and pulled back. Drunk on pleasure, he went to work on her skirt, tugging the stretchy material up her hips and out of his way. Then without so much as a "do you mind?" he snagged her underwear and pulled it clear down her legs and to the floor.

When he'd exposed every inch he wanted to see, he took her hand and held it against his compressed erection, tightening his hold on her hand so she was forced to squeeze his thick length. "Does your Duracell lover feel like that? Does he suck your nipples as hard and as long as you like, cara? Does he get you off like I do?" Instead of freeing himself and putting them both out of their misery, Dean pushed her hand away and took hold of her hips and jerked her to him.

He lined her soaked slit against his jutting bulge and pressed against her. "Tell me again that I want you out of my hair. I dare you."

"I…can't."

"Because it's not true. I always want you. Always." He pressed himself against her hot core, rubbing his covered shaft against her pussy as she undulated under him. The intense pressure felt so good, she couldn't help but moan and arch her hips, wordlessly begging for more. She ground herself against him, coating the bulge of his pants with her sticky juices.

The speed at which she fell into his embrace almost embarrassed her. Almost. But it wasn't enough for her to push him away. Not when this was what she wanted. In fact, the only thing that would make it better would be to have him inside her. Nevertheless, he knew her too well, knew how to touch her to bring her over the edge. One last hard push of his covered cock across her clit was all she needed.

Swallowing a scream, she threw her head back and tightened her legs around him as mind-blowing pleasure rushed over her. The climax hit her hard and fast, and she cried out, dropping down to her elbows to brace her weight.

Dean wasted little time. Before she'd even begun to come down from her orgasmic high, he scooted her forward a bit and went to work on his pants buckle and zipper. Creigh licked her lips and looked at him hungrily. This was the moment she'd been waiting for, the moment when he would finally make her his again.

With frantic hands, Dean pushed his zipper down, then reached in and took hold of his cock. He was in the process of pulling his dick free when her cell phone chirped. Dean froze instantly, and in unison they both turned their heads and gazed at her purse on the counter. Creigh barely remembered bringing the brown bag in with her, but there it was, bold as day. Neither of them said a word as the phone rang again and again.

It was like a bad dream. Creigh couldn't think of a worse position to be in or a worse time for someone to call. That thought, however, brought to mind the reason she was there, and unfortunately it wasn't to get fucked. "Harlow," she whispered.

The one word worked like magic to rouse Dean into action. "Son of a bitch." He cursed under his breath and whirled away from her. She watched him move to the sink and grip the edge like a lifeline. He was as taut as a bow, and she couldn't blame him one bit.

With trembling hands she sat up and fixed her bra and shirt, all the while keeping an eye on Dean, who was as still as stone and twice as quiet. A few strained seconds passed, with only the sound of their labored breathing and that of the persistent caller to fill the silence.

Unable to think of anything to say, other than *fuck, fuck, fuck*, Creigh eased down off the table and pushed her skirt back into place. While she repaired her clothing, Dean did the same, then walked stiffly to her bag and retrieved it for her. As he made his way back to her, she noted he hadn't buttoned and zipped up, only shoved his cock back inside his boxers. The long, thick shaft was as evident behind the denim material as it had been pressed against her heated sex.

Wordlessly, he handed her bag to her, then stepped back and winced, his hand immediately going to adjust his groin. He didn't attempt to zip his pants back up, and for that Creigh was thankful. It would be terrible for him to accidentally injure a cock as nice and big as his. Hell, she considered it a miracle he was able to stifle his large erection behind the wall of his boxers.

"Thank you." Creigh accepted her purse, then dug around in it for her cell. It took only a few seconds for her to find it, and when she did she glanced down at the number for a brief second to reassure herself they hadn't stopped in vain before pressing the Talk key.

"Hello."

"Mom." There was a long pause on the other end. "Is that you?"

Even to Creigh's own ears, her voice sounded strange. "Yes." She cleared her throat and tried again. "I'm here."

"Did you find it?"

"No, not at our house or"—Creigh glanced back at Dean, who was intently watching her—"your dad's."

"Aw man."

She could hear Harlow growing upset. "Did you save it on the computer? Maybe I can print up another copy."

"Mom, you're a genius."

Smart was the last thing Creigh was feeling right now. "I'll go home and print up a new one now."

"You're the best."

"I know." Harlow seemed so pleased. Well, that made one of them. "I'll talk to you later."

"Bye."

Creigh severed the connection and slipped the phone back into her purse before raising her head to stare at Dean. Their gazes locked, and Creigh licked her lips, still tasting him on her. If the phone had only rung ten minutes later, she could have slaked her unappeased lust on Dean's delicious cock. Just the thought of having him pound the walls of her pussy agai—

"If you don't stop looking at me like that," he warned in a dangerously soft tone, "I'm going to put you right back on that table and finish what we started, and to hell with Harlow's paper."

"No. Don't say that." Creigh's cheeks heated, but she looked away, not wanting them to get into any more trouble than what they already were. "She'll get a failing grade."

Dean let out a sharp bark of laughter that sounded far from amused. "Ask me if I care right now."

"One of us has to." Lord knew she was having a hard time making that person be her.

"Do you?" His tone dared her to lie.

It was a challenge she couldn't accept. Not when the truth was so evident. "I'm trying very, very hard to pretend like I do." Creigh bent over and picked up her discarded underwear. "I...I...have to go."

To her immense relief, Dean didn't try to stop her. Creigh didn't think she could have stayed strong if he did. Next to signing her divorce papers, walking out of Dean's house was the hardest thing she'd ever done. But then, just as now, she did it, regretfully and wondering if she was making the worst mistake of her life.

Dean pulled the car into the driveway of his old house and quietly cut the engine off. Staring up at the home where his family slept, played, lived, and loved without him wasn't easy. It hadn't been the other two times he'd come out this week or the four the week before or even the two the week before that. In fact, since their separation there hadn't been one week Dean hadn't made a drive-by to see his family. Sometimes he parked across the street and just stared. Others he just drove by slowly to make sure all was right in his loved ones' world.

Leaving the keys in the ignition, Dean picked up his cell phone off the passenger's seat and dialed Creigh's cell-phone number by heart. He cut his gaze to his wristwatch. It was only a bit after ten. She was more than likely still up. It took a few rings before she picked up. "Hello."

"Hey."

"Dean." Her voice was husky as if he'd wakened her from a deep sleep. That was strange. Creigh normally was a night owl. Maybe the new baby was making her tired. "Dean, are you there? I can't hear you."

"Yeah." Dean cleared his throat, then spoke up. "Sorry if I woke you."

"I wasn't sleeping."

Her reply brought back the other memory of the one thing that could make her sound all husky this late at night. "Did I catch you during? Or after?"

"I'm hanging up." He could hear her embarrassment over the line.

"Hmmm." Her nonanswer said it all. "Right in the middle. Nice."

"Maybe for you. But not for me. Being interrupted twice in one day is just cruel."

"At least you got to come," he reminded her softly.

"It wasn't enough."

"Never is." Dean looked up at the master-bedroom window that faced the street and smiled. "I remember how it sometimes took hours on hours of fucking just to get you to the stage where you could finally go to sleep."

Her breath hitched. "Saying things like that doesn't help."

Dean grinned. "Sorry."

"Liar. I'm surprised to hear from you."

"Did you really think I was going to let you escape from me after what went down in the kitchen?"

"Think, no." She laughed softly. "Hoped, yes. Things got out of hand."

"And you ran."

"And you let me."

"I don't think you would have been"—Dean paused, searching for the right word—"prepared for me to come after you. I was too riled up. Too tense. Five more minutes and I would have been fucking my frustration out on you."

"I think…" Creigh cleared her throat. "I think you mean taking your frustration."

"No, I said what I meant."

He heard Creigh inhale sharply before continuing in a much more subdued voice. "Then it's a good thing I ran."

"I'm not so sure about that. You running makes me want to chase after you and finish exactly what we started. And whether you want to admit it or not, it would have felt damn good."

"I'm woman enough to agree with you. Hell, Dean, we were always good in bed."

Dean thought of their children, nestled in for the night. "We did some of our best work there."

"Yeah, we did." Turning the conversation to their kids brought out a smile in her voice. "They're asleep, by the way, in case you wanted to talk to them."

"No, I called to talk to you."

"Me?" The surprise in her voice was a bit amusing.

"Yes, you." Dean leaned back in his seat. "In fact, why don't you just open the door and come outside, and we can finish this conversation face-to-face."

"Outside?"

"Yes, I'm parked in the driveway."

"Are you kidding me?" She gasped. Before he could reply, Dean heard the sound of her feet pitter-pattering across the creaky wooden floor. Seconds later the curtains parted, and Creigh's face appeared in the window. "What in the world are you doing here?"

"I wanted to see you."

"Mission accomplished."

Not really. As far as he could tell, there was only one lamp on in the bedroom, and it wasn't casting a very revealing light on her, much to his dismay. "I want to see more of you. Come out."

"It's the middle of the night," she reminded him unnecessarily. "The kids are light sleepers, remember?"

"Then you better be quiet. Also, keep on whatever it is you're wearing."

"What game are you playing?"

He smiled. "Come find out. Olly olly oxen free."

"Dea—"

He could hear her protesting, but he hung up nevertheless. He knew Creigh well enough to know she would be too intrigued not to come see for herself why he was there.

Less than a minute later, the front door swung open, and on cue Creigh stepped out and quietly closed the door behind her. Barefoot and dressed only in a long-sleeved, button-up shirt that reached midthigh, she quietly made her way over to the Impala. Her dark brown hair fluttered around her shoulders as she quickly made her way to him. She stopped in front of the hood and ran her hand over the new paint job that had his baby shining like spit-polished shoes. Shaking her head, she rounded the car to the passenger side. After giving a quick glance around her, she opened the door and climbed in.

"This is crazy. I can't believe you're here. In this, of all things." Reaching out, she rubbed her hand over the black upholstery he'd finally been able to refurbish three months ago. The smell of oil and leather filled the car, like in the good days when his dad owned it.

"You're really doing a good job on it." Her voice was a bit awestruck. "Your dad would have been proud."

"I like to think that." His dad had loved this car, and he'd passed that affection down to Dean, who hoped one day he could do the same to Hamilton. "Still a lot to do, a lot of money to pour into her before she's golden, but one day she'll be right as rain."

"I know she will. Does the heater work yet?"

"Yes."

"Mind flipping it on? Some of us are a bit underdressed." Creigh rubbed her hands over her bare thighs. The shirt she wore did little more than button up the front and hang several inches above her knee. All the bare flesh he could see made him hunger to look at the parts he couldn't see.

"So I see." Dean turned the car on and revved the engine for a bit before leaning over and then flipping the switch for the heater. Cool air followed by a faint hint of dust flowed from the vents for a few seconds before the warmth became noticeable. "By the way, that shirt looks awful familiar." Reaching down he fingered the green flannel shirt. "Very familiar."

Creigh smacked his hand. "They didn't break the pattern after they made yours, you know."

"Ouch," he said, shaking his fingers. "Hit me all you want. I know that's mine."

"Prove it in a court of law."

Dean's smile slid away. "I'm a little lawyered out, I have to say."

The amusement that had been brimming in Creigh's big brown eyes just moments ago quickly slid away. Sighing, she looked out the car window and into the neighbor's yard. "I don't want to fight."

"You took the words right out of my mouth." Dean said. "I'm done. I refuse to go another second dealing with it."

Creigh turned her attention back to him. Her eyes shimmered with unshed tears, but she held strong. "I understand," she said with a nod. "I want you to know, even though I haven't shown it all the time, I really do appreciate the help you've been in the last week. And I'll try my best not to bother you again."

How could someone so smart be so lame when it came not only to his heart, but hers as well? "Keep your thanks, Creigh. I don't want them. My actions weren't noble at all. I didn't do what I did this weekend for you. I did it for me. The baby was the first step I saw to possibly making my way back into our home, and I pounced. I kept telling myself you needed me. That you couldn't—no, shouldn't—do this alone, when in all reality, it's I who needs you."

"That's not true. I've always needed you. You've never needed me."

"That's where you're wrong. It scares me just how much I do need you. Do you know why I'm out here tonight?"

She shook her head. "No."

"Because the day ends in *y*." He smiled. "I come out here so often it's ridiculous. Pathetic even. Just in hopes I'll see one of you in the window or outside for a split second. Then there're the other times, like tonight when I know you're all in bed but I come by anyway, just to watch over you for a little bit. This is where I belong, Creigh, and I want to come back home."

"Things"—she paused to gather herself before continuing—"aren't that simple. No matter how much I might want them to be. You have no idea how badly I just wish I could take your hand and tell you to come home."

"Then do it." He'd come too far to be stopped now. "What's so complicated?"

"Everything. You're only doing this because you see me as a damsel in distress. If I hadn't gotten knocked up, you wouldn't be here, and I don't want to drag you back into a bad situation because you think being with me is the right thing to do."

"Hell, I'm not sure this *is* the right thing to do. All I know is I can't stand being without you. The baby is just giving me the push to do what I wanted to do. I never wanted the divorce. You know that."

"I also know that we were tearing each other apart. Do you really think we're so much different now than we were two years ago?"

"I know I can't go another year without you."

"I'm not the same person I was when we were married."

"Good. Come to find out, that person wasn't very happy, and I don't want that for you anymore. We'll both have to get to know the new us. I'm not saying I just show up tomorrow with my bags and big-screen."

"Then what are you suggesting?"

"That we go out on a proper date, several of them, and get to know each other all over again. Maybe we'll find there is something between us besides sexual chemistry; maybe we won't. But whatever we discover, it has to be better than the unknown we live with each day. I don't want to fight with you anymore. I don't want to be the dick that makes you cry all the time."

"And I don't want to be the bitch who sends you running for the garage to escape me."

"What do you want? We've said what we don't want."

"I want to be happy again. With you."

"I want that too." God, did he. More than anything else in the world.

"I want to be okay with still being in love with you."

"For the record, I'm okay with that," he joked around the lump in his throat. She still loved him.

"And I want you to be able to handle this." Creigh laid her hand down on top of her small yet growing bump. "God, I want that so badly."

"I can, cara." Dean cupped her cheek in his head, tilting her face up a bit so she could not only see into his eyes, but also hopefully his soul. "I want to make her my child. If you'll allow me."

"As wonderful as that sounds, there is a lot"—she closed her eyes for a second before opening them and continuing—"you still don't know."

"Then tell me."

She pulled away from him and turned her head. "I'm not ready."

Dean let out a disappointed breath. "What could be so bad it has you this upset?"

Creigh looked at him and met his gaze. "It's not what; it's who."

"The baby's father."

"Yes."

"Who is it? Is it someone I know?"

For a second, he thought she wasn't going to answer, but then she gave a sharp nod.

"And that's what eating you up inside. The fact I know this man."

"Yes."

"Tell me who he is. I can handle it."

She tucked a strand of her dark hair behind her ear. "I don't think you can."

He racked his mind to try to figure out who it might be. An old acquaintance, maybe one of the guys he saw on a daily basis. Through all the faces that popped in his mind, he couldn't mentally connect Creigh with any of them. "Well, I know she's not Sergio or Gino's child."

Creigh gasped, her face a mask of disgust. "Of course not. I would never. They would never."

"I know, baby." Dean laughed. "I was just saying my brothers are the only men who could bring me low, so if it's not them, the father doesn't really matter."

"Can I get that in writing?"

"Yes," he said with all seriousness.

"Before we go one step further, I think there is one more thing about the baby you need to know."

"Okay." He braced himself and waited for the news, hoping for the best but fearing the worse.

"She...she won't be like Hamilton or Harlow."

"What does that mean?" Dean reached out and placed his hand over hers, willing the unborn child to be okay. "She's all right, isn't she?"

"Yes, of course." Creigh moved her hand out of the way so his was lying flat on her stomach. "What I meant is her father isn't white. If we get back together, there will be no pretending you're the father. She won't look like you, at all. She probably won't look much like Hambone or Harlow either."

Insulted, Dean slowly pulled his hand away. "And you thought you had to tell me that? You thought it would matter?"

"I thought you deserved to know."

Dean thought about what she said for a moment and let it sink before he replied. He didn't want her to think he was answering off the cuff or hadn't thought about the possibilities and the ramifications for himself. "For the record, I didn't think you were catnip for white guys. I knew there was a chance the father would be black. Just like I'm hoping you know it won't matter a damn bit to me. I'm capable of loving a child for merely being a child, not for who her parents are. I'm bigger than that."

"I know you are," Creigh said sincerely. "I just thought you should know."

"Well, now I do."

Creigh stared at him for a second, gaze intent as if she was searching for the truth of his words in his eyes. What she saw must have appeased her, because after a bit she smiled shyly. "The next time you feel the need to drive by, maybe you should just get out and come in."

The offer meant more to him than he could say. "Maybe I will."

"Good. I would really like that." Creigh reached for the door handle. "It's getting late. I should probably head back in."

Oh hell no. Dean turned off the car. He wasn't going to allow her to get away that easily. Acting fast, he placed his hand on her thigh. "Or you can stay out here with me for a moment longer."

"I thought…" Creigh glanced down at his hand, then back at him. "I thought you wanted to try to get to know each other again."

"Tomorrow." Dean moved his hand from her thigh to the bottom button of her shirt and slowly began to undo them. "Tonight, you and I have a little unfinished business to attend to."

Creigh let out a shuddering breath but didn't make a move to stop him.

"They say the third time is the charm. Let's find out if they're right." As soon as Dean undid the last button, the shirt parted, exposing her bare flesh to his hungry gaze. Creigh was nude beneath the green flannel and just as breathtaking.

The outside light from above the garage door shone into the car allowing him to see every single inch of her exposed frame. Dean drank her in with his gaze. Without anything to obstruct his view, he could clearly see the evidence of the life growing inside her. Her usually taut stomach jutted out in the sweetest of ways, yet it didn't detract from her sensual appeal at all. It made Creigh look even more beautiful to him, womanly even.

"God, you're beautiful." His body was humming from the prospect of being with her again. No one, but no one ever made him feel as alive as Creigh did. She was the reason he drew breath in the morning and the reason he was here, putting everything on the line to be with her again. "How did I let you walk away from me?"

Creigh went to respond, but Dean silenced her with his mouth. His tongue slipped between her lips, and he pulled her closer to him. As sweet as she tasted, as good as it was to feel her mouth against his, it wasn't enough.

Not nearly.

After a few seconds of pulse-pounding kissing, he broke away from her tempting mouth, his breathing as out of control as the beating of his heart. "Open your legs for me, cara," he ordered huskily.

Creigh was a little slow to follow his command, so Dean did it for her. He pulled her legs apart and slipped his hand between her soft brown thighs, moving it slowly against her silky, soft skin until he reached her slick curls. Dean brushed his fingers through her dampness, seeking the slippery entrance to her sex. What he found there took his breath away. Creigh was blistering hot. Just the way he liked her. "Miss me?"

"God yes. I've been on fire since this morning." She moaned, undulating her pussy onto his seeking fingers. Dean allowed her a few seconds of pleasure before he drew his hand away and centered his finger against her clit. "No," she protested, turning wild eyes on him. "Don't tease me."

Dean ran his finger in circles around her erect little bud, hard enough so she could enjoy it, but light enough to have her craving more. "Would I do that?"

"Yes, you bastard."

"Give me what I want, then, and I'll give you what you need." This wasn't their first rodeo. He knew she was well aware what it was he was asking for.

Without a word of protest, Creigh sat up straight and quickly took the shirt off. She cupped her breasts in her hands and offered them to him. Her dark nipples puckered under the weight of his gaze, like two juicy blackberries. "Perfect."

Dean lowered his head and opened his mouth, taking one deliciously dark nipple between his lips, then tugged. Creigh arched slightly at his touch. She whimpered her approval and pressed even closer to him. His thumb sought her clit, rubbing it with sure deft strokes. Enraptured by her, he suckled at her breast, pulling her nipple farther into his mouth all the while steadily increased the pressure he was applying on her erect bud.

After he thoroughly laved the first breast, he moved on to the next one and ravished it in the same manner he had the other as she writhed beneath his touch.

If he had anything to say about it, she would feel his touch on her breasts for days to come. Dean wanted her to think of him every time she rolled over, every time she put on or took off her bra, every time any wisp of fabric touched her nipples. He wanted her to remember this moment, this time, his touch.

"Please"—Creigh released her grip on her breasts and slid her hand over to his lap—"I want to touch you too."

Dean couldn't have resisted her if he wanted to. Moving away from her breast, he made quick work of freeing his erection. The second he pulled himself completely out, Creigh knocked his hand away and took him in her own. The precum leaking from the slit in his crown made for excellent lube. Her soft hand explored his hard flesh, stroking him frantically at a pace that soon had him as crazed as she was. Her touch drove him wild. She knew his body as well as he knew hers, and it didn't take much for her to start making him see stars.

Seeing as how she had things well in hand, Dean moved his hand back between her legs and took up where he had left off, driving her out of her mind with pleasure. He began to pump his fingers into her with fast, furious strokes, grinding his palm against her clit.

Dean pulled her closer to him and buried his face in the crook of her sweet-smelling neck. There wasn't enough room in the car to take her the way he truly wanted, nor was he capable of moving to larger accommodations. They would have to take what they could and make the most of it for now, but later, later he would make up for tonight's rushed joining.

He moved his mouth from the haven of her neck to the small lobe of her ear and whispered in a lust-thickened voice, "Your pretty pussy is squeezing the life out of my fingers, cara. Makes me wish it was my cock buried in your sweet cunt."

Dean didn't think it was possible, but the walls of her sex clenched even tighter around him. Creigh undulated her hips toward his hand, taking his fingers deeper inside her. "Oh just like that, cara. Fuck my fingers. Show me how much you've missed my big dick."

"Dean, Dean." She moaned and rocked her hips back and forth.

"Oh yeah, cara. I can't wait to fuck you again." He pulled his fingers out of her briefly and used them to land a stingy slap against her tender clit before cupping her pussy in his hand once more and shoving three fingers this time into her hot cunt. He made his motions rougher, because he knew that was the way she liked it. A little pain went a long way to get his girl off.

Creigh cried out and jerked. "Fuck! Dean…oh…God."

"Liked that, did you, baby?" He reached over and grabbed hold of one of her nipples, pinching the turgid flesh between his fingers. Giving her that added bonus he knew would blow her mind.

"Yes. Yes." She whimpered, tightened her grip on him, and stroked him faster. She utilized her knowledge of him to give him the handjob of a lifetime, squeezing up, pumping down. She worked him over like a seasoned cock pro, all the while moaning and humping his hand.

"Your hand feels so good, baby." He groaned, leaning closer to her nipple, wanting—no, needing—to take her back in his mouth. "You make me feel so good. So fucking good."

Creigh did something with her thumb over his crown, and he was gone. Words were no longer a possibility for him. Just groans to show his appreciation. Creigh wasn't much better. She was tossing her head back and forth, her moans increasing tenfold. She was just seconds away from dousing his fingers with her sweet essence.

The scent of her arousal filled the car, the noise reached a decimal a pitch above ear bursting, and the windows fogged up from the steam generated between the two of them. It was like high school all over again, but worse because Dean knew what he was missing. And it was time he reminded her as well.

Closing his lips around the tip, he bit lightly into her nipple once more. The sharp bite was the catalyst to her undoing. Creigh threw back her head and screamed his name, soaking his hands with her creamy essence.

Dean was right behind her, or before her, he couldn't tell. It was definitely a photo-finish orgasm. Dean couldn't say if he shot jet after jet of semen out of his cock and over her clenched fist first or if she flooded his fingers first. All he knew was it was damn good. And messy. He was going to have the car detailed tomorrow, but it was worth it to have her in his arms again.

Chapter Six

"So, tell me."

Creigh looked up from the arrangement she was making for tomorrow's display to gaze at her cousin, who was staring at her intently. "Tell you what?"

"How it feels to be dating your ex-husband?"

"Ohh…that." After doing a quick check to see if Sergio, who was helping out in the back room, was nearby, she set one of the last flowers in the vase. After two months of seeing Dean again, there were only two words she could think of. "Frustrating and weird."

A-mei frowned. "That's not good."

"No, it is. I mean things are really good between us." Better than it had ever been between them. "And that's what's so weird. Neither of us are going into this with blinders on. There are still times I want to throw a pot of grits at him, but those are less and less. We're talking things out now. Before I would have stormed away and called him names, and he would mutter something I'm sure didn't mean 'my beloved' in Italian and slam the door. If he gets upset, he might step outside for a moment still, but now it's to grab me a flower from the garden to say he's sorry or to do something equally nice."

Smiling, A-mei hopped up on the table and picked a lily Creigh had yet to place in the vase. "Wow, sounds like he's really turning over a new leaf."

"He's trying. He really is." Creigh smiled at the memory that came to mind over the weekend. He'd caught her lifting a crib—still encased in the box—out the back of her car.

He'd wanted to rail—she could see it in every fiber of his being—but he'd kept silent and asked her in a very strained voice to go open the door so he could bring it in. When she'd stupidly began to argue, he'd sent her a look that could have frozen fire. In the past, he would have taken one look at her struggling to remove the box and just erupted. There would have been yelling on his part, cursing on hers, both just going at it until they were too worked up to even handle being in the same universe with each other. This time, he'd taken a deep breath, leaned the box against the car, then took her face in his hands and kissed her, putting all his frustration into the embrace.

If his goal at the time had been to circumvent an argument, it worked like gangbusters. The second he was done kissing her, Creigh was no longer thinking about him helping her with the baby furniture; she was thinking about him helping her act out how people got pregnant in the first place.

A-mei used the flower as a feather and rubbed it against her bare arms. Her cousin was a very tactile person. This wasn't the first time Creigh had caught her molesting the plants.

"Hey." Creigh held her hand out to A-mei, who smiled sheepishly and released the flower.

"Sorry, lost myself for a second. Back to you now. Have you told him about"—A-mei glanced down Creigh's stomach, then back up—"you know what, yet?"

Creigh busied herself to avoid the censoring look she knew A-mei would rightly send her way. "About being pregnant," she questioned in a flippant tone. "Yes, he knows."

"You know that's not what I mean." Leaning forward, her cousin lowered her voice. "Have you told him who the father is?"

Creigh looked away and didn't answer. The father of her unborn child was still something she'd prefer not to talk about. She hadn't spoken to him in months, and she didn't want to. In fact the only thing she wanted more than for him to disappear off the face of the earth was for his identity to be a nonissue for everyone else.

True to his word, Dean had refrained from bringing the subject up again, but Creigh knew it was still a sore point. It would be for her if the situation were reversed.

Her silence must have been answer enough. "Oh, honey." A-mei's face was sympathetic and completely nonjudgmental, which was why she and she alone was privy to the truth about the baby's lineage.

"I know," Creigh said with a deflated sigh. Nothing anyone could say or do could possibly make her feel any guiltier than she already did. "I know it's the right thing to do. I just…there just… The timing always seems wrong."

"Do you think it will ever feel right?"

"I don't know," she answered honestly. "I try not to think about. It's hard enough living in the now."

"And how's the now treating you?"

"Good, but frustrating." She went back to her first word of choice as she placed the flower in the vase.

"Why? It sounds like everything is going back to normal, or better than normal. What in the world are you complaining about?"

"I'm complaining because everything isn't normal."

A-mei's brow wrinkled. "Come again?"

"We're a bunch of grown-ass adults sneaking around."

"Sneaking around?" A-mei's eyes widened with disbelief. "You mean the kids still don't know you guys are seeing one another."

Creigh shook her head. "No, because we don't want them to get their hopes up in case we realize this isn't going to work after all. They've been through enough, don't you think?"

"Yes, and I can see why you think that. But where do they think you're going once a week when you go out? And who do they think you're talking to on the phone at all hours of the night?"

"They think I'm talking to you on the phone."

"Thanks for adding me to the web of deceit."

Creigh laughed but continued. "And they think Dean and I are going to Lamaze. The kids think he's agreed to be my coach."

"I thought you didn't start going to that until your third trimester?"

Creigh smiled sheepishly and picked up the vase. "They don't know that." She walked the pretty arrangement over to the floral cooler and set it in the last empty spot.

"So is that the frustrating part? Lying to the kids?"

After closing the door, she walked back over to where A-mei sat. With a pensive look on her face, she crossed her arms over her increasingly larger breasts and leaned next to her cousin on the table. "It's part of it."

"Girl, I keep telling you guilt is a useless emotion. And just think—you're lying to them now; one day they'll start dating and start lying to you. It's the circle of life, Simba. It's just the way it's supposed to be."

Creigh looked up at her cousin fondly. "A-mei, do me a favor."

"What?"

"Don't reproduce."

A-mei shuddered, as if the very idea gave her the creeps. "Girl, please. Having kids is the last thing I ever want to do."

"You know you just got yourself pregnant by saying that."

A-mei sighed. "Probably."

"Good thing you're not seeing anyone."

A-mei shot a quick look to the back room before nodding in agreement. "Yep. Good thing," she said, turning back to favor Creigh with a smile. "I guess I'll just have to live vicariously through you. So can I hear about what I'm missing out on?"

Creigh snorted. "Unless you want to hear about dinners, movies, walks on the beach, and shopping, then you need to turn your attention to someone else, because this girl"—Creigh pointed to herself—"ain't getting jack crap. We've even gotten to the part where kisses have been cheek centered and not lips."

"You're not"—A-mei lowered her voice and leaned in closer to her cousin—"fucking?"

"No." Creigh shook her head sadly.

"Oral or maybe some mutual masturbation?"

Ever since that first night in the car, they hadn't done shit. "Zip, zilch, nada."

"Why?"

Creigh shrugged her shoulders and turned around to face the table. She begin to clean up the mess she'd made, all the while thinking over the question A-mei put toward her. Yet the few extra seconds didn't give her any more answers than the seconds before that. "Honestly, I don't know."

"But you must have a theory?"

That she had. In boatloads. "Maybe he's trying to be a good guy and not rush things." Any more than they already had. "We did say we needed to learn to communicate outside the bedroom."

"That makes sense."

"Yeah." But that wasn't the theory that kept her up at night. "Or…"

"Or?"

"He couldn't be physically attracted to me in my condition." At six and a half months pregnant, Creigh was a lot bigger than she had been at four. It was almost as if she'd tripled in size. Even her doctor was giving her the side eye and had her on a carb-light diet. Even though it pained her to admit it, she wasn't exactly bringing the sexy right now.

"Girl, please. I can't even count how many times I've caught the two of you going hot and heavy when you were pregnant with the other two and much further along." A-mei shuddered. "I learned my lesson the hard way. I don't care if you did give me a key. I will never just walk into your house, never ever again."

"It wasn't that bad." Creigh tried hard to keep her amusement at bay.

"For you, maybe, but not for me. There are some things that once seen can never be unseen, and trust me, I've witnessed enough freaky shit to know that's true."

"I'll take your word for it."

"Then take it for this too. Dean is crazy about you. You should see the way his face lights up when you walk into the room. I can't imagine why you think all of a sudden, because your belly is poking out a bit more, he isn't into you."

"If he is, then why haven't we made love?" Creigh asked.

"Maybe because he's leaving it up to you." A-mei hopped down from the counter and faced Creigh. "Have you said, 'Dean, make love to me'?"

Of course she hadn't. "No."

"Okay, then." A-mei's face turned serious. "This is what you're going to do. You're going to take the kids to your mom's house tonight; then you are going to find a sexy maternity negligee—"

Creigh rolled her eyes. "That's an oxymoron for so many reasons."

"*And*," A-mei stressed the word, as she always did when she was overriding anything someone said. "You're going to invite him over to dinner. When he asks what you're having, you say pussy, then climb up on the table, pull up your gown, and spread your legs. If he's not over there on the floor before you can get 'bon appetit' out, something is wrong."

"You have the dirtiest mind of anyone I know," Creigh said, but with a smile. Leave it to her pervert cousin to get her out of her funk.

"And the freest schedule of anyone in the world. If you want to get this little experiment in the works, you should head out early so you can get back in time from dropping your kids off."

Eyes wide, Creigh stared at her cousin in shock. She was serious. "You don't mind closing the store again, even thought it's not your turn?"

"Not at all. That's what cousins are for."

Creigh stared at her for a second, weighing the pros and cons. Then common sense kicked in and put her ass in gear. "You are so right. I owe you a massive one." She pulled her cousin into a quick hug. "I need to go pull the kids out early and take them home to pack."

"Then you better get to it."

"I am." She smiled at A-mei. "I'm out." Acting quickly, Creigh gathered her things from behind the counter and hightailed it out of the store before A-mei could change her mind. Talking to A-mei had really put things into perspective for her. Either she was going to get laid or she was going to find out why.

* * *

"Guess what?"

Dean looked up from the coffee machine in the break room and over to his coworker with a bored expression on his face. He didn't want to play guessing games. Dean just wanted to put in his 7.5 hours and get the hell out of Dodge. It was a feeling he'd been dealing with a lot lately since he'd been promoted to management.

A suit-and-tie kind of guy, Dean wasn't. He'd even turned the job down the first time Roland Sparks offered it to him. Dean was more comfortable working on the floor with the boys than sitting in some minuscule little room making schedules and crunching numbers. But Roland wouldn't hear of Dean turning down the position and had used the magic of the almighty dollar to do the convincing for him.

"I said, guess what, man?" Buckley repeated a bit louder.

"What?" Dean said at last as he poured in a generous amount of creamer into the white coffee cup the kids had gotten him last Father's Day. It read in big blue print, *When God created fathers, He said let there be love.* It was Dean's favorite and sometimes the only thing that helped him make it through the day. "What's the news of the day?"

The ruddy-faced, heavyset man came closer and lowered his voice. "Elvis has entered the building."

Dean groaned. The nickname brought only one person to mind, Trace Sparks, Roland's son. "No. Say it isn't so."

Buckley wiggled his upper lip in a poor intimation of Elvis, the nickname they'd given Trace for his kinglike behavior. "Uh-huh."

"Fuck," Dean groaned, not happy at all to hear the news. He couldn't stand Trace; the feeling was more than mutual. "When and for how long?"

"Rumors are 'the king' is finally taking his rightful spot as heir."

The last bit of happiness he had hidden deep, deep, deep inside his soul slipped away. Man, it was time to go home. "How's Roland taking it?"

"Old man is as happy as a lark."

He is the only one. After all these years and everything they'd been through together getting over the death of Dean's parents—who also happened to be Roland's best friends—Dean thought of Roland now as his friend. And it was the immense respect Dean had for Roland that forced Dean to keep his mouth shut and not let the older man know just what a wastrel piece of shit he'd fathered. He loved Roland too much to break the other man's heart, but if there ever were a bigger waste of space than Trace, Dean never had the displeasure of meeting them. "Are we sure he's not just here for his monthly lording sessions?"

Trace was a fan of rubbing what he considered his birthright in the face of the men and women who actually made the cans that bankrolled his elaborate vacations and made his carefree life possible. Normally Trace was only in town long enough to check in with his doting parents before whisking away again. Then there were the rare occasions when he actually stayed for a few months to get a refresher course on the company. Dean was seriously hoping Trace was here for the former and not the latter. The last thing he wanted was the little rich kid poking his nose in Dean's office, offering sage advice on something Trace knew nothing about.

Even growing up, the two men never got along. It wasn't anything that had improved with age. With a growl, Dean rustled his hair. "If I ask you nice enough, will you shoot me and put me out of my misery?"

"You don't have to ask me nicely at all," said a deep voice from behind them. "It's the least I can do for such a good friend."

Wouldn't it fucking figure. Not only was he back, but was in spitting distance, breathing Dean's recycled air. "No, the least you can do is nothing. And we're not friends," Dean said casually with his back still turned to the other man as Buckley fumbled around, his mouth opening and shutting like a gasping fish trying to find the right words to fix this. Dean, on the other hand, didn't want to fix dick.

He wasn't going to give Trace the satisfaction of a stumbling apology. If there was one thing proven time and time again, eavesdroppers never hear any good about themselves, which in Trace's case wasn't that all surprising. There was nothing good about him.

"Dean. Dean. Dean. Now why would you want to say something so mean? After everything we've been through together, shared together, you think we'd be on at least friendlike terms."

"Think again." Dean turned around to face the other man, but on his terms and in his time. With coffee cup in hand, he leaned back against the sink and took in Trace, who was leaning against the doorjamb, hands crossed over his chest. As usual, the dark-skinned, handsome African American man wore his usual my-shit-don't-stink smug expression. It coordinated perfectly with the suit that was way too expensive and out of place in a cannery facility. But Dean knew Trace thought dressing for success would impress the low men on the totem pole. He was wrong. It only made them dislike him more.

"Nice to have you back, Trace. You going to be here long?"

Trace turned his head to face Buckley and said, "Uh-huh." His impersonation was far better than Buckley's and twice as funny since it could only have meant he overheard the two men talking about him.

That suited Dean just fine. He thought it was about time someone knocked Trace off his high fucking horse. Buckley on the other hand looked as if he'd swallowed his tongue. "I...uhh...I..."

His stammer seemed to amuse Trace, who grinned and walked into the room. "No worries." He slapped Buckley on the back as if the two of them were old friends. "I can take a joke as well as the next person, but don't you have a line you need to go check on?"

"Yes, sir. Right away."

Buckley scampered from the room as if the hounds of hells were on his trail. Dean watched the entire encounter with cool amusement as he sipped his coffee. It was official—

Buckley had caught Trace's attention. His days at the plant were numbered. Pity. Dean had always thought he was a nice enough fellow. As soon as Buckley was gone, Dean turned to Trace. "A line to check. You don't even know what he does here."

"I was giving him an out he so desperately needed. That was me being kind."

"No wonder I couldn't tell."

"So I'm the king, huh?"

"That's the way you act." Dean made his way over to the sink to pour out the rest of his coffee.

"Says who? The haters."

Dean rinsed out his cup and sat it upside down in the dish drainer before turning and facing Trace once more. "As far as you're concerned, haters come in two characters. Type As are the ones jealous of what you have and who you are. Buckley might fall into that category, only because he hasn't been here long enough yet to become a type B, which I'm a proud member of."

"And what type would that be?"

"Type Bs simply…" Dean tilted his head to the side. "Hate you."

"I think the type Bs are the ones who are the most jealous."

Dean laughed, unable to help himself. "Trace, I can assure you. You don't have anything I want. Never have. Never will."

"Never say never, Dean."

"Never," Dean said emphatically.

Trace watched him with a smug look in his eyes. "We'll have to put that to the test sometime."

"Wonderful," Dean said drily. "I can't wait. Oh wait, yes, I can." Bypassing the other man Dean left the break room and headed back to his office. His assistant, Vivian, was on the phone, but the second he walked to her desk she told the caller to hold and moved the phone down a bit and covered the receiver. "Creigh called. She said it wasn't anything urgent, but when you had the time to call her back."

"Thank you," Dean said, a bit amazed. Creigh never called him at work unless there was a problem, and even though she said there was no rush, he couldn't help but worry. After hurrying into his office, he shut the door firmly behind himself, then made his way over to the phone on the desk.

Dean didn't even bother to sit. Instead he dialed her cell number from memory and prayed everything was okay. It only took a few rings before she picked up, but by then he'd worked himself into a fine state. "What's wrong?" he barked the second she answered.

"Dean?"

"Yes. Is everything okay?"

"Everything is fine." Her voice sounded as calm and as stress free as a warm summer day, instantly putting him at ease.

Letting out a deep breath, he sat in his chair and said a quick prayer of thanks. "I was worried about you. That maybe something had happened today."

"No, everything is fine. I…uh…wanted to know if you wanted to come over for dinner tonight. That is…if you don't have any other plans."

"Other plans?" He chuckled lightly. "Sweetie, you and the kids are my only plans. Ever."

"Good. Would you like to come over for dinner?"

"I'd love to." If anyone would have told Dean six months ago Creigh would be inviting him to break bread with her and the kids, he would have called them a liar and probably punched them in the head for getting his hopes up. But these days, things were going so well, he didn't know what do. Dean was so afraid of fucking it up again that he was going beyond the call of duty to make sure he did everything right. "What time would you like me to come?"

"Is six too late?"

"Not at all." She could have said now, and he would have just walked out the office and made some bogus excuse. Truth be told, though, he was happy he had some time to go home and shower before he went to see her. Showers were the only thing saving his mind the last two months. Well, not the showers, per se, but the jerking off he did while in there to prepare himself for being face-to-face with the woman he wanted more than his next breath.

Masturbation wasn't keeping the beast down; it was just appeasing it a bit and helping Dean with his quest to show Creigh they could be about more than sex. "Yeah, six is good. Gives me time to clean up before I get there. Do you want me to bring something?"

"Just you."

"I can do that." Dean paused for a second, then lowered his voice. "I love you."

"I love you too." She sounded shy, but she'd said it, and that was all that mattered to him.

Chapter Seven

Creigh took one look in the mirrored closet doors at her reflection and gave a halfhearted smile. The black-and-white floral strapless shirt she wore together with the jean skirt that fell several inches above her knees and the black wedge sandals wasn't exactly a cock-hardening negligee, but it would have to do. There was only so much sexy she could bring with a basketball-sized late-night snacker growing in her womb. She could only hope it was enough to garner Dean's attention.

She needed to get laid and in the worst way possible. As Dean had predicted, her Duracell lover was not holding up to his end of the bargain. Maybe she should have went with Energizer, the lover that would keep going and going, because what she was working with now in her California Exotics Clitorific vibrator didn't seem all that clitorific these days. Sure, she was coming, but her orgasm in no way matched the intensity of what she experienced in Dean's arms.

Just thinking about their brief encounter two months ago gave her the tingles all over. She could only hope tonight ended on a similar note. Lord knew she needed it. Creigh realized things were bad when she began eyeing the arms of the couch as a potential outlets for her pent-up desires. Before she could dwell too much on her out-of-control libido, the doorbell rang, ending her musings. Startled, Creigh glanced over to her nightstand and noticed the time. It was a few minutes before six.

He was early.

Creigh turned her attention back to the mirror and gave herself a quick once-over, then took a deep breath. Ready to take on the world, she smiled encouragingly at herself, then hurried from her room to the front door.

"Think sex. Think sex." She whispered the mantra to herself as she unlocked the door, then pulled it open. Portraying more courage than she felt, Creigh placed her hand on her hip and smiled invitingly. She pushed the security door open and stepped into view.

"Oh...wow..." Dean's widened eyes spoke volumes as his gaze ran like a lover's caress slowly over her body, taking everything in from her bone-straight hair, parted down the middle, to the plush curves of the top of her breasts to her French-pedicured toes. Dean took his time drinking her in, and when he finally raised his gaze back to hers, his eyes were filled with an unmistakable heat so intense it took her breath away. "You look...beautiful."

His frank approval sent her ego soaring and brought the long-buried seductress out of her. "Thank you." Creigh stepped back to allow him to come in.

With his gaze still running rampant over her, he shut the door. "Did I misunderstand? Are we going out?"

"Why? Would you have changed into your good jeans?" she teased, giving his casual outfit of jeans and a T-shirt a quick perusal. His clothing wasn't fancy, but as usual, Dean looked damn good.

"I might have put on a belt or something."

Creigh laughed softly. "You needn't get fancy. We're staying in."

A slow, sexy smile spread across his sensual lips. "Lucky me."

Creigh felt his words to her core, and it made her tremble. It was just something about the way he said it that made her feel like the lucky one. Fuck yeah, she was getting laid tonight, even if it meant she had to push him down and ride him like a bucking bull to accomplish it. Trying to get her head back on track, she blurted out the first thing that came to mind. "Would you like something to drink?"

"A beer if you have it."

"Of course." At least these days. Since he'd been coming by more often, Creigh had slipped back into the habit of picking up a six-pack when she went to the store. She knew he enjoyed a good cold one every now and then, and it pleased her to have them there for him. It was the small things that mattered, and she hoped he saw her actions for what they were—Creigh trying to make him feel more at home. In hopes that maybe some day soon, he'd start thinking it was his home again. "I'll go get you a bottle. You can wait in the living room if you like."

"You don't have to wait on me. I can grab it."

"Dean." She smiled indulgently. "It's a beer. I think I can handle it." With a roll of her eyes, she turned and headed toward the kitchen.

"Fine," he said from behind her. "I'm being overprotective. Message received."

Grinning, Creigh glanced over her shoulder to find Dean following her into the kitchen, his gaze glued to her rear. For all his faults, he was good for her self-esteem. Now if only she could figure out why he was keeping her at arm's length. It was becoming increasingly obvious he didn't find her newly expanding waistline repulsive. So why was he holding back?

Creigh pondered that question on her way to the kitchen. The scent of the pot roast cooking in the oven hit her the second she entered the overly warm Tuscan-inspired room. If she would have thought of this wonderful plan this morning, she would have put the meat in her Crock-Pot before she went to work and saved herself the added heat, but since Creigh planned for them to spend the majority of the time in the cool bedroom, she wasn't overly concerned with it.

Before grabbing the beer, she checked on dinner. A blast of heat struck her in the face when she opened the wall oven, as did the delicious aroma of the browning meat and potatoes.

"Mmm, pot roast," Dean murmured from behind her. "My favorite."

"I know," she said with a smile, as she closed the door. "It just needs a little bit longer." Like an hour or so longer, and she knew just how they could spend that time. After adjusting the oven temperature, Creigh walked over to the refrigerator and opened the door. She looked around for a few seconds, then bent over slightly to grab the longneck bottle from the bottom shelf. When she stood and turned around, Dean was right behind her.

He was so close, she could feel the heat radiating from his body. Nervous, she offered him the bottle. He took it but didn't bother to open it. Instead he lowered his hand to his side and stared intensely at her. "Where are the kids?"

Creigh wet her lips and stepped away from the refrigerator, letting the door close behind her. She walked over to the counter and leaned on it for support. "At my mother's house."

"For how long?"

"Till morning," she admitted almost reluctantly. The closer she came to the point where she knew she was supposed to be bold and tell him what she wanted, the harder it was to meet his gaze. It was so much easier picking her outfit than it was plotting how to convince him to make love with her.

"Hmmm..." Dean stepped a bit closer to her and set the bottle on the counter behind her. His arm brushed against hers in the process, and the simple touch caused goose bumps to break out across her arms. Damn, she was in serious need of some loving. "Why do I get the feeling that this isn't a mere coincidence?"

"Because it isn't." Creigh rubbed her arm to calm her flesh and to keep her idle hands busy and away from Dean's too-tempting jeans.

"Interesting." He took yet another step closer.

His nearness had her head spinning and pussy clenching. Dean's presence was going straight to her head. Reaching out behind her, she grabbed the counter for support and willed her voice to stay even. "What's so interesting about it?"

"You." The way he was watching her so keenly began to wear on Creigh, and her courage began to slip away. Maybe this wasn't such a good idea after all. Who was she kidding? She wasn't a siren. She wasn't a seductress. She was a pregnant mother of two.

"You don't have to stay if you don't want to." Willing to give him an out if he needed it.

"Oh I want. Desperately so. I just want to know something first." Dean placed his hands on either side of her on the counter, trapping her inside his arms. "Are you trying to seduce me?"

Creigh forced herself to hold her head high and met his gaze. "I have no idea what you're talking about."

Dean leaned in closer, so his lips were mere inches away from her ear. "Don't you?" His whispered words played like fingertips across her nipples.

"No," she breathed, trying desperately to hang on to the little bit of strength she had left.

"Then the new outfit, the freshly done hair and nails"—Dean lowered his head a few inches, then leaned in even closer to her neck and inhaled deeply—"and that scent. The sweet heady perfume of yours you know I love. It's merely a coincidence." He raised his head and focused his punch-drunk gaze on her. "And it was in no means meant to drive me out of my fucking mind."

Well, when he put it that way. "Maybe." Creigh wet her lips. "A little."

Dean moved so quickly he startled her. He pressed against her and wrapped his arms around her. Creigh could feel the growing bulge of his erection against her. Dean wasn't immune to her after all. "Just a little?"

"Maybe a bit more than a little."

"How much more?" Dean wrapped his hand in her hair and tugged her head back.

As much as Creigh would have liked to pretend that his caveman ways did nothing for her, she couldn't. His actions, the predatory way he watched her, the domineering way he held her, had her juice creaming her thighs.

He tightened his grip. The added pressure made her gasp, not in pain, but in need. "Tell me."

"A lot," she finally whimpered.

"Good. Consider me seduced." Dean used his grip on her hair to hold her steady, then covered her lips with his.

Creigh's eyes closed automatically, and she surrendered to his embrace. She kissed him with all the hunger and passion in her soul. Groaning, Dean responded in kind. He used his free hand to pull her flush against him. Her belly prevented her from pressing fully against him, but she greedily and happily took what she could get it. She lost herself in the sensation of his kiss, the thrill of his touch, and she knew, despite how desperately she wanted to make love to him, she could have settled for just this. Being with him in any intimate way again.

After a few moments of sheer bliss, Dean lifted his mouth off hers. He let out a shaky breath and rested his forehead against hers. "You're making this hard on me."

Boldly, Creigh worked her hand between them and cupped his erect cock. "Lord, I hope so."

"Cara." The rough desire in his voice made her pussy clench. "I'm trying so hard to be good."

"Don't," she whispered. "I like it when you're bad."

Dean pulled back a little bit and stared intently into her eyes. "And all that stuff you said about talking and getting to know each other better?"

"Right now, there's only one part of you I want to get to know better."

To her utter surprise, Dean lowered himself to his knees in front of her. "Only one?"

She stared at his mouth with a hunger she could never describe. She'd obviously misspoken. "Or maybe…or maybe two."

Dean reached up under her floral shirt and took hold of the stretchy material of her maternity jean skirt, and tugged. With very little effort the skirt gave and ended up as a dark blue puddle at her feet.

Since none of her underwear was even the slightest bit *un*-grannylike, Creigh had decided to go sans panties, which left her wearing only her shirt, her wedge sandals, a spray or two of perfume, and the thin layer of cocoa butter she'd rubbed onto her skin after her shower.

"Hold on to something." It was the only warning she received before he lifted one of her legs and placed it on his shoulder.

"Dean!" Creigh reached behind her to the counter and gripped it with all her might. Without waiting to see if she did as he'd ordered, Dean spread her slick folds apart and buried his mouth in her pussy. His tongue flicked over her soaked slit for a few seconds before he took her clit between his lips and sucked the hard nub with an intensity that made her weak in the knees.

"Oh, God... Dean..." Creigh wanted to entangle her hand in his hair and pull him even closer to her, but she knew if she let go of the counter, that would be all she wrote. She was forced to surrender herself to Dean's talented tongue and leave the driving to him. As keyed up as she was and as skilled at pleasing her as Dean was, it didn't take Creigh long to come.

Her body barely stopped trembling before Dean stood and kissed her deeply. She welcomed the taste of herself on his lips and tongue. Just as she welcomed the man himself back in her arms and life.

With a shudder, Dean pulled back and stared deep into her eyes. "I want you," he murmured huskily. "Missed you so damn much."

"Missed you too."

Before she could say more, Dean bent down and picked her up as if she weighed less than nothing and carried her the few feet from the kitchen back into the living room. He did it with a grace and strength that startled her and made her feel all kinds of womanly. If she hadn't wanted to fuck him before, after that smooth move, she would have gladly dropped to her knees and shown him her appreciation. Even though she enjoyed his Clark Gable impersonation, there was a freshly made bed with their name written metaphorically all over it.

"The bedroom…" She gestured toward the room with a slight nod.

"Is too far away." He set her down in front of the couch and began to undress.

Creigh undid her shoes, then unhooked her strapless bra from beneath her shirt. After freeing her breasts, she flung the bra off to the side but chose to keep her shirt on, and by the time he was undressed, she was more than ready to pick up where they left off.

Dean sat on the couch, and Creigh instantly climbed on top of him. She held on to the back of the couch for leverage as he scooted down a bit for comfort. This was a position they'd mastered during Harlow's stay inside Creigh. Girl on top gave Creigh all the power and comfort she needed during this stage, but it also gave Dean and his wandering wonderful hands lots of opportunity to reach and touch her anywhere and any way he liked. A win-win position if there ever was one.

Greedy and ready to have him once more, she reached for his cock, desperate to have him inside her. To her surprise, though, Dean smacked her hand away. "I don't think so. Give me what I want."

Creigh knew exactly what he was implying, so she didn't waste time arguing. She pulled her shirt down to the top of her stomach, allowing her breasts to tumble free. The second they were out, Dean was on them. Cupping them in his hands, he took his sweet time teasing and tormenting her nipples with his mouth and fingers. If it hadn't been for her orgasm earlier, Creigh was sure she would have gone mad with hunger, because although his cock was more than hard and ready, inches away from her pussy, Dean refused to thrust inside her until he sated his never-wavering lust with her breasts. This too was a sexual tradition she knew well.

Normally, Creigh would have enjoyed nothing more than having all this attention paid to her sensitive mounds, but right now she was hungry for cock. She was so desperate, she found herself rubbing her pussy back and forth against his dick as he suckled and pinched her nipples roughly.

Soon she had his cock so slick she was gliding across him, her clit on fire from the stimulation, but there just wasn't enough pressure there to get her off. "Jesus, please, fuck me." Creigh groaned. "Please, baby. Fuck me."

Dean released his grip on her breasts and moved a hand down to the flesh of her ass and delivered a well-aimed smack. Creigh gasped, and her pussy soaked his cock with the evidence of her desire. There was nothing that turned her on more than when Dean took charge in the bedroom. "Ahhh…fuck."

"Been so long you've forgotten your place?"

"No." She shook her head. "Never."

"Then where is it?" He delivered her twin cheek the same punishing smack he did the first.

"Under you, over you, surrounding you. Wherever, whenever you say."

"Then why are you rushing me?"

"Because I need you. So fucking bad."

"Need me." He flexed his cock from beneath her. "Or my dick."

Creigh refused to lie. She was too desperate to have him in her to do that. "Right now, I need your dick."

"Such a greedy bitch."

"Your bitch."

"Damn straight." Dean reached between them and pulled his cock back until it was poking up. He ran his thumb across his damp crown, then brought his finger up to her mouth. "Is this what you want?"

Creigh parted her lips, licked off his salty essence, and moaned. "God. Yes. Please."

"My pretty baby knows what I want to hear, then?"

Yes, she did. And she did it with pleasure. "Fuck me, *caro*. Fill me with your cock."

"Such a dirty little girl."

"And you love me."

"Every inch of you."

Creigh rose to her knees, grasped his cock, and with Dean's help centered it against her slick slit. Carefully she lowered herself, taking much of the turgid length into her. It took a few attempts to get him in as deep as she liked, but when she did, it was golden.

Pausing to take in the moment, Creigh dropped her head back and let out a deep breath. Dean held himself still inside her. His lack of movement allowed Creigh to relish the heady sensation of being joined with him once more. She was home. At last.

Sitting up, she placed her hands on Dean's shoulders and used him as an anchor to help her rise and fall on his well-slicked shaft. "Dean…" Creigh tightened her hold on him.

"Cara...ride me." He gripped her ass cheeks in his hands and began to rock her back and forth on his cock.

It had been so long since she'd been filled, she almost felt out of practice. But Dean was there with her every step of the way, supporting her, fucking her, giving her everything she needed and more.

Creigh worked herself on his cock, fucking him with all the passion and love inside her. As she moved, Dean shifted one of his hands closer to the split of her ass until his fingers rested lightly between her cheeks. He ran them up and down her crack, seeking but not asking for more. After a few seconds of the maddening play, when she offered no resistance, he became bolder, dipping the tips of his questing digits into the crevice between her firm half globes.

There had never been a part of her body Creigh had held back from Dean, and she wouldn't start now. She welcomed his touch against her crinkled hole, welcomed it even more so when he slipped his hand underneath her as she rose, and coated his fingers with her dew.

With his fingers now slick with her cream, Dean moved back to her rosette and began to lightly circle around her nether hole, alternating between light caresses and gentle presses until he had her moaning for more. "Do it," Creigh pleaded, wanting to be filled any and every way by him. "Don't stop now."

"Never."

Creigh leaned forward, which spread her ass apart a bit more and gave Dean all the leverage he needed to slowly and tenderly ease his middle finger partially inside her. Her downward thrust did the rest, sinking him even deeper into the recesses of her ass. And when she rose again, Dean pulled back but then pressed forward, filling her bottom as surely as he was filling her pussy.

The addition sent her soaring. God, she'd missed this. Missed him.

"That's it, baby; take all of me."

There were no words to describe what it felt like being fucked so good and hard by him. Creigh pushed down, grinding herself harder on him as he pumped his cock inside her, finger fucking her ass all the while.

After that, speaking became unimportant. Their groans and moans became their own personal love song as their voices grew louder and louder with every thrust. While she busied herself fucking Dean raw, he leaned forward and took a turgid nipple into his mouth, sucking it with the tight pressure Creigh craved.

Creigh tossed her head back and cried out at the added pleasure. He was trying to kill her. From the breasts to the pussy to the ass, then back to the breasts. It was the kinky fucking circle of life, and it was driving her wild.

"Oh oh oh oh." She was in another world, her eyes shut tightly, her breath coming in little gasps. Creigh was coming undone, and she was so close to climaxing she could taste it.

As if sensing her impending release, Dean released his grip on her hip and let his hand fly, sending one sharp smack into her plump cheek. The unsuspected slap sent Creigh over the edge, and she screamed her release, flooding his cock with the essence of her passion.

Creigh collapsed on top of him, her body quaking with the aftershocks rocking through her. She didn't have the strength to hold herself up so he could finish, but luckily for him, Dean did. Removing his finger from her ass, he took her hips in both hands and worked her up and down on his cock, one pump after another until he tossed his head back and came, releasing a torrent of seed inside her waiting sex.

After several moments, Creigh turned her head so she could see Dean. He was looking at her too, with a look of tenderness she hadn't seen in a while on his face.

"You okay?" he whispered. Dean moved his hand from her hip to her hair and lovingly caressed it as he peered up into her upturned face.

"I feel…as if I can fly." A soft smile turned her lips upward at the corners. "I have to say, I'd forgotten how good in bed you were."

"I promise you won't have the opportunity to forget again."

Creigh's smile broadened and she closed her eyes, snuggling as close to him as she could. That was a promise she was going to make sure he kept.

* * *

After resting for a bit, the two of them showered together, then ate the meal Creigh had prepared. Dean couldn't help but notice it was his favorite, and he loved her even more for taking the time to make it for him. In fact, if he had to pick, there was only one thing about tonight's little festivities he wasn't enjoying. And that was Creigh's desire to keep her body clothed.

Yes, the outfit she wore earlier had been sexier than hell, but nothing in the world compared to Creigh nude. After their shower the only item of clothing he'd put back on was his jeans. Creigh, on the other hand, had changed into a royal blue strapless ankle-length maxi dress, which in his mind meant she was vastly overdressed.

The truth of the matter was, this hidden shit wasn't working for him. And although Dean was campaigning to bring his family back together on the "I'm no longer a dick" party, he could feel his asshole flag beginning to rise once more.

She was hiding from him, and that just wouldn't do. If it was the last thing he did, he was going to find a way around all her barriers. Making things right with her, really right with her, was the one thing besides their kids he was living for, and he was willing to do anything to make that happen. Well, anything but let her hide from him.

Despite being desperate to do whatever it took to get in her good graces, Dean could not be untrue to who he was either. Yes, there were parts of himself he was willing to change, no, willing to work on for her, but he would not and could not change who he was at the core. And that person wanted his woman to trust him enough to love her clothed as well as unclothed.

Not willing to pick a fight just yet, Dean let it go for now and tried his best to just live in the moment. After cleaning the kitchen, they returned to the living room and settled down on the couch to watch a movie. Dean arranged himself behind a lounging Creigh, with one leg against the back of the sofa and the other slightly bent with his foot on the floor. It was a position they'd taken up on the couch many, many times in the past, and it held a ring of familiarity that made Dean smile. It was as if their routine had never been broken. As if they'd never been apart.

Nostalgia wasn't the only emotion filling Dean. So was arousal, as it normally did when Creigh was pressed against him. The familiar scent of her skin, her hair, her body tantalized Dean's senses. Despite making love just a couple of hours earlier, he was as aroused as ever. The very idea of sliding his cock into her liquid heat had his balls aching and his dick growing hard.

Dean inhaled deeply, taking in her sweet fragrance and letting it fill his lungs and soul. Hungry for the taste of her again, he leaned his head down and brushed his lips against her neck.

Creigh gasped at his touch and tilted her head, allowing him better access to her. Smiling, Dean peppered her neck with his kisses, stopping only to pull up and whisper in her ear. "Do something for me?"

She turned her head and looked up at him at an angle. "Anything."

"Pull your dress up and play with your pussy for me."

Her face flushed. "Wow, so not what I thought you were going to ask."

"But you'll do it just the same, won't you?" Dean reached down and grasped a handful of the blue material on her thigh and began to pull the dress up slowly, exposing inch after inch of sexy brown skin. "You'll make yourself come for me just because I ask."

Creigh took hold of her dress and pulled it passed her knees, then butterflied her thighs. "What do you think?"

"I think you're a dirty little girl."

"Who likes to please her man."

Her man. He liked the sound of that. "One of your best qualities, hands down." His voice grew husky. "Now touch your pussy and make yourself come."

Creigh released her dress and slipped her hand between the juncture of her thighs. She didn't bother to pull anything out of the way which only meant one thing. "No panties, baby?"

"No."

Fuck, she's hot. "Hmmm." He closed his eyes, briefly picturing the thought. "I like that."

"I knew…" She paused, breath halted as if she'd touched on something worth touching. "Knew you would. I kept them off for you." From his position behind her, he couldn't see exactly what it was she was doing with her hands, but if her moans were anything to go by, it was something good.

"Are you wet, baby?"

Her eyes were dark and heavy lidded. "Why don't you touch me and find out?"

"Because if I touch you, I'll fuck you. Now answer me," he ordered, his voice rough and thick with his arousal.

"Yes. Soaking wet. My fingers are slipping and sliding all around my pussy."

Dean groaned at the image she brought forth and cursed their positions. He wished he could watch her brown fingers slip deep inside her warm pink flesh. He wanted to watch her tickle her clit firsthand, but since that was impossible because of the way they were sitting, he would settle for the next best thing. "Paint me a picture with your words, cara. Tell me what you're doing. Talk dirty to me."

"I...I'm caressing my clit. It's slick from my cream and so erect. Sensitive to the touch."

"Are you pressing on it lightly?"

She shook her head. "No. Rubbing with hard strokes. So turned on, it won't take me much to come."

He knew that feeling well. "What will it take?"

"Fingers," she gasped, moving her hand lower. "Fingers in my cunt."

"Then do that. Fuck your juicy pussy." Her nipples showed like pencil erasers through the thin fabric of the dress. The small beads called to him, and he couldn't, in all good conscience, ignore them. Tugging on the mesh material of her dress, he pulled it down and freed her luscious breasts to his waiting hands. And while she fingered her pussy, Dean toyed with her nipples, squeezing and pinching the pebbled peaks.

Aroused and intrigued, he watched her hand move and her firm thighs flex as she pleasured herself. The dainty little moans she let slip from between her half-parted lips let him know it wouldn't be long before she came.

"That's it, baby," he whispered in her ear, squeezing her nipples even tighter. "Finger that sweet snatch of yours and pretend like it's my dick buried in you again. If you come like a good girl for me, I'll bend you over and fuck you so hard. Make you scream so loud. Would you like that? Would you like my dick inside you again?"

"Yes." She whimpered. "I want you to fuck me so bad."

God, so did he. His cock was hard enough to bust through steel. It was taking everything out of Dean not to rub himself off against her delectable ass, but he refused to go out like a callow youth. He wouldn't come until he was buried deep inside her. "Then come for me, cara, and give us what we both want."

The words had barely left his lips before Creigh arched her back and cried out his name, shaking and trembling against him as she came. But she wasn't the only one affected by round two. Dean was breathing roughly and ready to pop like the fucking weasel. He was so close to coming he feared one quick move on her part and he'd be spraying his load on her back. And that was in no way how he planned to end the night. Not at all.

Taking her hands from between her legs, he brought her slippery, dew-coated fingers up to his mouth and cleansed them one at a time with his tongue, licking up the creamy evidence of her desire.

Damn, she tastes good.

"Something tells me we're not going to see the end of the movie." Creigh panted.

"What movie?"

She laughed. "Exactly." Sitting up, she turned around and ran her hand across the turgid length pressing against his jeans. "Want help with that?"

His cock jerked beneath her hand. Yes, he did. The thick, rigid proof was right there for the world to see. "Do you even have to ask?"

"I was hoping you'd say that." Creigh moved her hand to the button, but Dean gently pushed her hand away.

"Not out here." He picked up the remote and turned the television off. "Let's take this to the bedroom. I'll lock up, then join you."

Creigh stood and sent him a sultry look. "Don't be long."

"I won't." Hell, he was half tempted to say fuck it and take her on the couch again, but Dean wanted a little more room to maneuver this time. "Be ready for me when I get in there."

"Oh I will be."

He was counting on it.

It took only a few minutes for Dean to pull his car into the driveway and lock it, then lock the house down for the night. On his way to the bedroom, he couldn't help but think about how right this was. The only way it could have felt any better was if he was checking on the kids real quick before slipping down the hall to take his rightful place beside Creigh once more. But that was coming. Never had he seen the truth of that fact more than he did right now.

Unbuckling his pants, Dean entered the bedroom with only one thing on his mind. Fucking Creigh into the mattress. But the second he saw her propped up on the pillows with the quilt tucked under her armpits, he grew aggravated.

Normally seeing her on the king-size slat bed would have made him excited, but the way she had the covers wrapped around her like a mummy had him seeing red. She might feel the need to be wrapped up, but he didn't feel the same necessity. Dean unzipped, then pushed his pants down to the floor, stepping out of them when they puddled on the floor at this feet. His erection was pointing away from his body. "I thought I told you to be ready for me."

"I am." Creigh pulled back the covers on what used to be his spot and patted the mattress. "Get in."

"No. How about you get out"—Dean walked over to her side of the bed, then reached for the blanket and pulled it, along with the sheet, off her body—"from under the quilt so I can see the woman I'm making love too."

"Dean." She sat up and grabbed for the sheet. "You can see me just fine."

"I don't think so." With a flick of his wrist, he sent the covers flying to the foot of the bed, beyond her reach and out of his way. "I like them better down there."

Creigh rose to her knees and grabbed a pillow from behind her and turned it horizontally in front of her stomach, using it as a shield to cover her waist. Her large brown breasts lay on top of the pillow, and her eyes were alight with anger. Man, she was beautiful, but she was still going the right way for a spanking.

"Stop it," he ordered, irritated she felt the need to cover herself in his presence. Dean was willing to bet he knew her body better than she did. He'd seen parts of it before she had, been more intimate, more personal with her body, so much so, he arrogantly considered her body his. He was smart enough not to tell her that, of course. He was sexist, not stupid.

"Stop what?"

As if she didn't know. "Hiding yourself from me." Dean snatched the pillow away from her and dropped it on the floor. "If you're serious about us moving forward, you have to get over this."

Creigh placed her hands over her belly, her face flushed with embarrassment. "I wasn't... I just..." She stumbled over the lie, too honest for her own good.

"You were just hiding." He pushed her hands gently away and replaced them with his own. "Don't you know, cara? This is as familiar to me as that scar on your leg you received from falling on glass when we were kids." Dean began to rub her belly gently in circular motions. "As familiar to me as the tiny mole above your lip and the way you hum just before you drift into a deep sleep."

"You might be familiar with the casing." She reached down and cupped her hands over his. "But not the gift inside."

That made absolutely no sense to him. "Why is this gift any different from the two before it?"

Her eyes were somber, as if she was still waiting for the other shoe to drop. "Because she isn't yours."

Not this shit again. Dean sucked in a deep breath in an effort to keep his temper in check. Blowing up because Creigh still wasn't 100 percent sure he was going to be able to accept things was no way for him to prove to her that he'd changed. "But she's yours," he said firmly and with as much conviction as he could. "And that's all I need to know in order to love her."

Creigh looked down at their hands on her belly. "I bet you think I'm silly for worrying about this."

"Not silly, but it's not necessary. I love you." Dean moved his hand from underneath hers and cupped her cheek in his hand, gently forcing her to meet his gaze. "And I love her, and I want to take care of both of you. Not because I have to, not because you need someone, but because I love you and it pleases me to do for you."

"A few months ago, you saying you want to take care of me would have sent me running in the opposite direction."

"We're not the same people we were then."

"Is that good or bad?"

Dean took his hand down and answered honestly. "I think good, because of where we are now."

"In bed, naked?"

"I meant in our relationship," Dean corrected with a smile. "But naked in bed is always good too. Speaking of nakedness..." Since they were obviously in talk mode and not fuck mode, Dean figured he might as well get a little something cleared up. "We didn't use a condom earlier. Everything happened in the heat of the moment, but I should have still made an attempt to suit up."

Amusement curved the edges of her mouth. "You worried about getting me pregnant?"

"No, I just want to alleviate any fears you might have," he said, meeting her gaze head-on. They hadn't discussed their time apart since the night she told him she was pregnant, and he didn't want them going further with things if there was something she might have been worried about in the back of her mind. "When we were apart, I—"

Creigh covered his lips with her finger. "Dean, you don't have to say anything."

Dean moved her hand out of the way. "I do." For his peace of mind as well as hers. "I was careful. I used protection every time, but since we both know accidents happen"—he glanced teasingly down at her belly—"I want you to know I went and got tested last month. Everything is fine, but if you want me to use something…from here on out, I will."

"I had my doctor run tests too, and other than you know, the bunny dying, everything else came out fine. As for you wearing something, I think we've had enough between us to last a lifetime. I don't want anything else. Just you."

"Then you have me."

Creigh climbed from the bed, then took his waning cock in her hand and smiled. "And I know exactly what I'm going to do with you."

Her smile was purely sensual. Gone was the bashful woman from just moments earlier; in her place was the wanton woman he adored. "I like the sound of that."

"Then I'm willing to bet you're going to like the feel of this even more." Creigh grabbed a pillow from the bed and tossed it on the floor at her feet, then slowly lowered herself to her knees in front of him on top of the cushion.

From her position on the floor and the promise swimming in her eyes, Dean was willing to bet she was right.

Chapter Eight

"So is this your way of ending arguments from now on? Sucking my dick."

She could think of worse ways to say I'm sorry. "If it pleases you, I'm sure we can make some sort of arrangement."

"Oh it pleases me." He hurried to assure her. "It pleases me a lot."

Creigh could tell that just from looking at his hard shaft. A few minutes ago she would have sworn they were done for the night, but one touch of her hand and a simple change of her position had Dean's cock standing at attention and raring to go. The drops of precum beading on the tip of his thick weeping crown made her mouth water in anticipation. She couldn't wait to take him between her lips again.

"You going to stare or are you going to suck?"

Someone was impatient. "Can't I do both?"

"Not today." Dean took his cock in his hand and gave it a few strokes. "Right now I want your mouth."

"Bossy."

"Cara." Dean entangled his hand in her hair and took a step closer to her. Close enough the plum-shaped head of his cock was pressed against her lips. "Open your mouth and suck my dick."

Put that way, she couldn't refuse. Creigh pulled her head back a bit, fighting his hold on her just so she could get in the right position. While maintaining eye contact with him, she slipped her tongue out and lapped at his slick crown. "Hmm…"

"Tease." He tightened his grip on her hair and guided her closer to his cock. "You're a cruel, cruel woman."

"With the mouth of a saint." She closed her lips around his shaft and instantly became lost in the taste of him. All desire to tease and torment him fell to the wayside as Creigh tightened her lips around Dean's cock and familiarized herself with him once again.

After his initial attempt to control her movements, he relaxed and allowed her to suck him. Taking her time, she took him deep into her mouth before slowly pulling back, then sinking down once more.

"Fuck." Dean let out a deep groan as she swallowed the length of him. "I don't think saints do this."

She could live with that, she thought as she pulled back to the crown, then plunged down once more. She repeated the same cycle two more times, making sure to get his sex nice and wet before adding her hand to the mix. Dean enjoyed the double pleasure of a handjob combined with a blowjob, so she gave it to him. Milking his cock with firm, sure strokes, she followed her hand movements with her mouth, sucking and polishing his knob until his knees began to tremble and curses began to tumble out. Before she could progress too far into the groove of it, however, Dean entangled his hand in her hair once more and pulled her off and away from his spit-slicked cock.

"Get up," he ordered her huskily, reaching down to help her to her feet. As soon as she was standing on her own accord, Dean crushed her to him and covered her mouth with his.

Creigh moaned into Dean's mouth and wrapped her arms around him, wanting—*no, needing*—to be as close to him as possible. Her tongue danced over his, sharing with him the heady taste of him that drove her wild. And from the way Dean was frantically running his hands over her back and ass, Creigh could tell she wasn't the only one frenzied.

With a last lingering kiss, Dean broke the embrace and stepped back. "On the bed."

He didn't have to tell her twice. Creigh immediately turned and climbed into bed. She lay back against the pillows, curious to see what he had in store for her next.

"Up on your knees," he said hoarsely as he stroked his still-erect cock. "And scoot back to the edge. You know how I want you."

She did indeed. One of their favorite things about the bed was its height, which enabled Dean to fuck her long and hard for hours on end while standing without having to bend or arch up on his tiptoes. It put her pussy and, depending on how she situated herself, her ass at the perfect angle for him to fuck her deep. Just the way they both liked.

With a wicked smile, she moved to the center of the bed and positioned herself on all fours. She carefully scooted to the edge of the bed until her toes were hanging off, then reached over to the head of the bed and grabbed a pillow. Turning it on its side, she tucked it under her armpits and leaned forward. The pillow gave her a little extra cushion on her chest as she braced her upper weight on her folded arms. When she was all set, she glanced over her shoulder at him. "I'm ready."

"So I see." Dean moved himself behind her. Spreading the lips of her pussy with his cock, he stroked her clit with his slick crown.

Groaning, Creigh opened her legs wide for him and canted her hips in blatant invitation for him to enter her. "Please. Please. Please."

"So eager, cara." Dean gripped her hip in one hand and guided his hard cock to the entrance of her pussy. Pressing forward, he slid slowly inside her tender flesh. Creigh bit her bottom lip and groaned as her body stretched to accommodate his thick member. It was a tight fit, tighter than it should have been after their very vigorous round only hours ago, but Creigh didn't let that stop her from bearing back on him and taking his cock as deeply as she could into her welcoming warmth.

"Mmm, yeah." His fingers clenched her sides as he went in deep and he went in hard. She bit back a moan of lust. "Feels good. So good."

"Feels like coming home."

"I hope you're not *coming*"—she put an extra spin on the word to let him know she was teasing—"home too soon."

"No, cara, for you, I'll go all night."

The idea of fucking for hours on hours just didn't appeal right now. Creigh wanted fast and rough. It didn't have to be pretty. It didn't have to be sweet. All she wanted to do was to come around his cock and have him spill his seed inside her. Creigh didn't think she was asking for too much. "I don't want all night. I just want it hard and fast, and I want it now."

He flexed his hips, eliciting a groan from her. "Then brace yourself, baby, and I'll give you everything you desire." Dean placed one hand on her lower back, the other on her hip. He began a steady yet intense rhythm inside her that damn near drove her out of her mind with pleasure. Creigh could barely tell if she was coming or going; all she knew was she'd never felt this alive before in her life.

"Oh yes. Yes." Her words soon blended into inaudible sounds as he pounded into her. Gripping her tightly, he pulled her back onto him and pushed into her, causing her ass to smack into his pelvis with every thrust.

Over and over he powered into her body, fucking her with wild abandon. He was relentless, just the way Creigh craved. His forceful mastering of her body drove her closer to orgasm with every thrust of his big cock.

"This is what you wanted, right, cara?" He thrust even deeper as he spoke. "My cock, fucking you hard and good."

"Yes. God yes." Creigh pumped her hips, meeting him thrust for thrust without shame or worry. The angle they were in was perfect; it enabled Dean to take off the kid gloves and fuck her the way they both loved. She'd never felt so aroused in her life, or so loved. "Give me your cock. Fuck me. Fuck me. Dear God, fuck me."

There was a fierce passion to him that only came out when they were lost in the moment like this. The smack of his flesh against the flesh of her ass rang out louder than their moans.

"Dean," she sobbed his name, milking his cock with the contractions of her pussy as she came. Her orgasm triggered his, and with just a few pumps, he released a torrent of seed inside her.

Trembling, Dean leaned forward and rested his head on her back. Creigh released her death grip on the pillow and blindly reached back for him. She touched his arm and squeezed, letting that simple gesture do the talking for her, because he had literally fucked the words right out of her. Apparently there was a first time for everything.

* * *

Creigh heard them before she saw them, but she couldn't believe her ears. Sitting up in bed, she glanced with horror at her alarm clock. It wasn't even eleven in the morning yet. Her mother had offered to watch them until midafternoon. Ten forty was nowhere near midafternoon.

"Fuck." Creigh quickly got out of the bed and grabbed the navy blue maxi dress she'd worn for a little bit last night off the floor and slipped it on. Rushing to the bathroom, she threw the door open and shouted, "They're back early," then slammed the door quickly, praying Dean could sneak out the bathroom window before anyone was the wiser.

Shaken she made her way to her bedroom door. *This is not happening. It can't be.* She wasn't ready for—

"Mom, we're home." Harlow's voice preceded her by mere seconds as Creigh's daughter came barreling into Creigh's bedroom with Hamilton and Creigh's mother, Ginny, hot on her trail. The kids were exuberant, and for a moment Creigh wondered if the two of them had been too much for her mom, but one look at the slightly amused expression on Ginny's lovely brown face allayed that fear. Her mother didn't look as if she was running away from the kids out of frustration. In fact, given the *Looney Tunes* scrubs Ginny was wearing, it appeared as if the only place she was running was to work.

As if reading her thoughts, Ginny shrugged her thin shoulders. "Sorry. The flu bug is going around."

"Yeah, I know," Creigh said, rushing over toward them in hopes of shepherding them out of the bedroom before Dean appeared out of the bathroom. "Thanks for watching them while you could. Let's go into the living room and—"

"Is Dad here?" Hamilton demanded before Creigh could move them even one step in the right direction.

"Here?" Creigh asked, trying to buy herself some time. Good Lord, she was so unprepared for this. Although Dean and she had been seeing each other for the last couple of months, she'd never come up with a plan for how to break it to the kids if they decided to continue their relationship. The decision was officially now coming back to bite her in the ass.

"Yes, his car is out front," Harlow said, as if Creigh didn't know. "Are we going to his house for the weekend?"

"Yeah, are we?" Hamilton asked, hopping up and down like a Mexican jumping bean. "Are we?"

"Uhh." Creigh couldn't think that fast. Dean hadn't mentioned taking the kids to his house for the weekend, but truthfully other than the random "fuck me, fuck me, oh yeah," not much had been discussed last night. Her plans for the evening were ones more of action than those of talking. "I'm not sure."

"Well, where is he?"

"Yes, dear," her mother chimed in drily. "Tell us."

Creigh shot her mother a withering look. Ginny wasn't exactly helping the situation. Something she didn't think was entirely accidental. Her mother had never kept her feelings about their divorce to herself. In fact, Creigh was pretty sure Ginny never had an opinion she didn't share, whether the person she was annoying wanted to hear it or didn't. Her verbal swiping of late had been directed solely at Creigh, who Ginny believed was following in her own footsteps by marrying and divorcing young.

True, her mother had separated from Creigh's father before Creigh had even been born, but Ginny wasn't one for seeing the forest for the trees. All she knew was Creigh was making a big mistake by pushing Dean away. If there was anyone who would be more pleased that the two of them were reconciling, it would be the smug dark-skinned female version of Chuck Woolery standing in front of Creigh now. "Where is," Ginny continued, "my favorite former son-in-law?"

The bathroom door opened, and Dean spoke from behind Creigh, much to her dismay. "I'm here."

"Dad!" Harlow gasped as she looked over Creigh's shoulder toward the bathroom.

From the look of shock on her mother's and the children's faces, Creigh just knew this wasn't going to end well. Sighing, she turned around and spotted him standing in the bathroom doorway, wearing only his jeans and a smile. His dark hair was damp and spiky. Despite the very tempting picture he made standing in the steam-filled doorway, irritation filled Creigh for a brief second. *How is it possible that a man who normally wears two shirts everywhere can't find one to put on now?*

Hamilton was the first to recover, his astonishment giving way to pleasure a lot quicker than Creigh thought hers would have if the situation had been reversed. Hell, there were parts of her that were still stunned, and she was the one who'd been seeing Dean for the last couple of months.

"What are you doing here, Dad?" Hamilton bypassed Creigh and went to his father's side. Even though his voice was heavy with confusion, joy filled his soot-covered face. "Fixing something?"

Dean ruffled Hamilton's curly hair and smiled welcomingly at Harlow as if the kids finding them together was an everyday occurrence. "No. I was here visiting with your mom."

"And you decided to take a shower?" Harlow asked, slowly joining her brother at her father's side. Unlike Hamilton's, her face wasn't filled with joy; instead there was an edge of hope creeping into the smile slowly rising.

"Well, that is what I normally do in the morning when I get up."

Creigh's mouth dropped open as Harlow squeaked, "Get up?" her smile zooming past slow straight to beaming.

"Oh dear," Ginny said from behind Creigh.

That wouldn't have been the exact phrase Creigh would have gone with, but it was a start. A start to something she was in no way talking about right here and right now. She needed to get things back on her home court and far, far, far away from the bed she'd just made love with Dean in less than fifteen minutes ago. The scent of their union still lingered in the air and on her body, since she'd yet to shower, unlike Dean.

Taking a deep breath, she faced her brood and the problem head-on. "Before we start with the twenty questions, Harlow and Hamilton, go unpack your bags in your room; then head into the kitchen for breakfast. Your father and I were about to go down and make something." Well actually, the plan had been for him to make something while she lounged about in bed like the Queen of Sheba, but somehow Creigh didn't think that was going to happen anytime soon now.

"But, but..." Harlow's shock had obviously robbed her of coherent thoughts.

"No buts." Dean gave their daughter a light tap on her rear. "Go get started. There will be plenty of time for questions later."

"Fine," she grumbled. "Come on Hambone."

"'Kay."

Harlow led a disgruntled Hamilton out of the room, pausing long enough at the door to peer back at them inquisitively. Creigh could tell from the sour expression on her face that Harlow wouldn't be happy until she knew exactly what was going on. It was a look Ginny was wearing as well, but unlike Harlow, Creigh knew her mother wouldn't leave the room without an explanation or without giving her opinion on what was going on, no matter how much Creigh might want her to. Sighing, Creigh made her way back to bed and sat on the edge. If she was going to receive a lecture, she at least wanted to be comfortable.

"So," Ginny said once the room was clear of the kids. "What's going on here?"

Before Creigh could open her mouth to reply, Dean walked over to her side and placed his hand on her shoulder. "I think it's pretty self-evident," he said calmly.

"I'm not so sure about that."

"Mom." Creigh just wanted to get this over with. "Don't overthink it. It's not a big deal. Divorced couples hook up all the time."

"Hook up?" Ginny's brows rose almost to her hairline. "I thought you said he wasn't the father?"

"He isn't," Creigh said at the exact same moment Dean said, "I am."

Startled, Creigh turned her head and looked up at him. "Dean." He gazed down at her, and his eyes were filled with a bit more amusement than she thought the moment called for. "Not helping."

"What?" He didn't seem the slightest bit put out by the flat-out lie.

Was he really going to pretend...with her? "You don't have to—"

Dean squeezed her shoulder. "It's better we just get this out in the open now." Dean looked back at Ginny. "Creigh and I are getting back together, and we're going to raise this child together. Case closed."

Creigh felt as shocked as her mother looked. They hadn't talked about the future, at least not to this extent. "Dean—" she whispered faintly.

"And the father?" Ginny asked, riding roughshod over Creigh's faint words. "What about him?"

"You're looking at him," Dean said, his voice taking on an edge as if he was daring Ginny to contradict him. "I'm the father."

"I see." To Creigh's amazement, Ginny smiled. "I knew there was a reason you were my favorite former son-in-law. Or is that changing too?"

"None of your business, Mom." Creigh knew if she didn't put her foot down now, her mother would never back down. And there was no way such an important decision would be made right here and now without Creigh even having an input in it. "Thank you so much for watching the kids. We can take it from here."

"Well, if I would have known he was the reason I was doing it, I might have tried to keep them longer." She shrugged with regret. "As it is, I have to drop and run. Someone called in sick at the hospital, so I have to cover their shift. I wasn't looking forward to going in early, but now I have to say I'm happy I did. I would have missed the big reveal if I would have waited."

"When there was something to announce, you would have been the first to know," she lied. Her mother would be in the top five but not the first to know.

"I'm not even going to comment on that blatant fib. No need hurting my feelings." Ginny wiggled her fingers in a good-bye wave on her way out the room, leaving Creigh and Dean alone in her wake.

Creigh shook her head. "Wow, that wasn't awkward at all."

"I didn't think it was so bad." Dean leaned down and brushed his lips against her forehead.

Where the hell has he been? Creigh turned on the bed and looked up at him. "It's only the beginning, you know. Everyone is going to be talking."

"Let 'em talk. As long as they do so respectfully in front of you and the kids, I don't really care what they say."

"Speaking of the kids, I think we need to get a few things cleared up." *More than a few.*

"Like?"

"Like what we're going to tell the kids." She couldn't believe he was being so blasé about everything. "I mean it's one thing to just blurt out to my mother that we're getting back together and raising the baby with one another, and quite another to explain the situation to Harlow and Hamilton."

"We'll tell them everything they need to know and not a word more." Dean spoke as if no further explanation was needed.

"And what's that?"

Dean smiled indulgently. "That we love each other and we're getting back together."

"And by back together, you mean dating."

"I mean us remarrying and me moving back home."

Creigh gasped. "Remarried!" Suddenly their relationship seemed to be moving at the rate of a speeding train.

"Yes." He met her stare levelly. "Why are you so surprised?"

Eyes wide, she stared at Dean as if he'd grown two heads. Surprised? Why wouldn't she be surprised? Marriage was a big step, an even bigger one the second time around. "Because we haven't even discussed that."

"What did you think all of this was leading to?"

He had a good point. Nevertheless, she'd been too busy enjoying their time together to envision what the future would hold. "I...I honestly don't know." Creigh slowly rose to her feet and took a few steps away. She needed room to breathe. Space to take it all in.

"Talk to me," he said gruffly.

"It just seems like it's all happening so fast," she said, turning to face him.

"Patience has never been my strongest attribute."

"Neither is being subtle."

"Are you saying you don't want me to move back in? You don't want to remarry? You don't love me the way I love you?" Dean spoke calmly, but there was a thread of steel underlying his questions.

"No, of course I'm not saying that." Creigh was more in love with him today than she ever was. There were many things she was unsure of, but her love and her desire to be with him wasn't one of them. "I think I'm just in shock. It's not every day someone proposes to me."

"You didn't get proposed to today either," Dean reminded her.

Taken aback by his reply, Creigh furrowed her brow. "But…but…"

"I may be an insensitive jerk sometimes, but even I know better than to do it like this."

Creigh couldn't help but laugh. What a jerkface. Here she was getting all worked up about moving too fast, and he could put the brakes on. Narrowing her gaze, she stared at him, lips quirked up in a half smile. The big faker. She was willing to bet he'd said what he said the way he did just to freak her out a bit. "You're such a jerk."

"Hey, I have to be me." Dean held his arms out wide.

"Fine, then"—Creigh crossed her arms over her breasts—"if this wasn't a proposal, then when are you thinking of asking me?"

"At the right time," he taunted.

"Which will be…"

Dean arched an eyebrow. "Now who's being impatient?"

"Ugh, you're such a—"

"Mom, Hamilton's being a pest," Harlow shouted from the living room, interrupting Creigh midrant. Before either Creigh or Dean could reply, Hamilton hollered back, "Mom, Hamilton's being a pest," in his best Harlow impersonation.

Dean put his arm around her shoulders. "We need to go before they kill each other."

"Are you serious? You're going to drop the marriage bomb and then just go?" Creigh felt as if her head was still swimming with everything that had happened in the last few moments.

"Pretty much."

"You're...evil." Shaking her head, Creigh uncrossed her arms and placed one around his waist.

"I know." He winked. "But you love me anyway."

He was right. She did.

* * *

Life was good, Dean thought as he twisted the top off of his soda and leaned back in his office chair. Very good. Normally Dean was a half-empty sort of guy. He wouldn't have put the word pragmatist out there, but for a large part of his life he acknowledged if someone else were to say the world on whole sucked big donkey balls, well, Dean wouldn't have been one to disagree too loudly.

These days, though, life was going good, and not just things between him and Creigh. Lord knew that was going all sorts of right, but now that the kids were in the know and now that they had both agreed moving back in together and getting remarried was the endgame, all Dean could see was a glowing future in store for all of them.

The only down part of his day was the fact Trace was still hanging around at work. It really did look as if the other man was here to stay this time. And as much as Dean hated him, even Trace's presence didn't weigh him down too heavily. Besides, Dean was beginning to think it was time he remade his entire life, not just his love life.

And the first step was to find another job. There were a couple of local plants that would offer him a nice signing bonus to hire on with them, but Dean would never do something like that to Roland.

Hands down, his boss was one of the best men Dean ever had the pleasure to know. He couldn't remember the first time he'd met Roland. The older man had been around long before Dean had even been thought about. In fact, outside of work, Dean called Roland uncle, as did his brothers and sister and all their kids. That was just how close they were to the other man, and just why it was going to be hard as hell to just walk out on him.

The sense of loyalty Dean felt toward Roland went beyond the boss-employee relationship. They even transcended play-uncle boundaries. And that was because Roland was all those things and more. The older man and his wife had stepped in when Dean's parents passed away and helped cut through the red tape with the life-insurance policy, making sure it was divided up squarely among the four kids.

Then as if that weren't enough, he'd lent Gino the money to start the bar, and a few years later paid for Annabelle's wedding and given her away. Added to that, Roland was renting Dean the house he was living in for a price so low it was ridiculous, and he was paying for Sergio to go to school. Roland and his wife were so ingrained in their family, Dean felt as if by leaving, he would be running out on the man who had been like a father to him over the last dozen or so years. Which made the very idea of working elsewhere ten times harder. Dean couldn't stomach disappointing a man who'd gone beyond the call of duty for kids who weren't his own. But truthfully, Dean didn't think he handle being there much longer either.

Whatever he was going to do, he wanted to do it soon. The baby would be here in a few weeks, and he wanted his house in order before she came.

She.

Dean smiled at that. Baby H, as he'd teasingly called her, was making her presence known more and more each day. From her kicks and elbow presses, he could already tell she was as strong as her brother, and from the way she had Creigh on a schedule already, he could see she was going to be as demanding as her sister. Then there would be qualities that were distinctly all hers that would make getting to know her even all the more exciting.

Two weeks, and all the waiting would be over, and their family would be complete once more. Not that he was waiting on her birth before he made good on his plans to marry Creigh. Oh no, that was happening sooner than she realized, when she least expected. He'd been planning the surprise proposal for a while now, and with the help of the two most devious women he knew, A-mei and his sister, his plan was going to go off without a hitch this weekend.

Dean was beyond ready for her to wear his ring again, and he was hoping Creigh would agree to make it nice and legal as well before Baby H made her debut. Then, once everything settled down, he planned to approach Creigh about finally revealing the name of Baby H's donor so the three of them could come up with a legal understanding. From the lack of interest the man had shown so far, Dean was willing to bet it wouldn't take much to convince him to sign on the dotted line and relinquish his parental rights. Once the deadbeat dad was out of the way, Dean planned on adopting baby H.

It was all a lofty plan, and of course it was contingent on many things. But Dean's motto was "go big or go home."

In the midst of Dean's rumination, there was a soft knock on his door. "Come in," he called out. Sitting up, Dean placed his soda down on the desk next to his uneaten lunch.

The door opened, and Creigh peered around the frame. "Hi. Am I interrupting?"

"Not at all," he said with a smile, rising from his seat. Dean rounded the desk and was halfway across the room to her before she barely had time to close the door behind her. Happy to see her and wanting her to know it, Dean took her in his arms and locked his hands behind her back. He covered her lips with his own and kissed her, with all the passion and desire he felt inside.

Things were just getting good when, with a soft laugh, Creigh pulled back and looked lovingly up into his eyes. "If I didn't know any better, I'd say you're happy to see me."

"Always. To what do I owe this lovely surprise?"

"I had a delivery in the neighborhood, and I thought while I was over here, I'd take you out to lunch. Seems as if I arrived just a few minutes too late."

"Not at all. I haven't even taken a bite. I can just pack it back up and have it for dinner."

"Or," she said, playing with his lapel, "you can throw it away and just have dinner at home, followed by breakfast, then lunch, then dinner again."

Home. Damn that word sounded good. "Is this your way of asking me to spend the night?"

"Tonight and every night. It's time, don't you think? It feels…" She paused as if she was searching for the accurate word. "Right."

"Yes, it does." Although he'd originally planned to move in right before the wedding anyway, it was nice to know she was as ready for him to come back home as he was to go back.

Creigh opened her mouth to say something but was cut short by a rapid heavy knock on the door seconds before it was pushed open.

"Dean, have you…" Roland paused in midsentence when he caught sight of Creigh and smiled. The jovial African American man came into the room with a big grin and shut the door behind him. "Well, well, well. Look who's here. Creigh, come give me a hug, girl. I haven't seen you in forever."

Creigh left Dean's arms and went into Roland's, who hugged her gently before stepping back and looking down at her. "You get lovelier every time I see you."

"And you get more silver-tongued. How are you? How's Sharon?"

"We're fine. Fine." Roland slipped his arm around her shoulders and walked her back over to Dean. "Dean told me the two of you had reunited, but apparently he left something out." The older man pulled away from Creigh and slapped Dean on the back good-naturedly.

"I did not." Dean had spoken to Roland about them dating months ago. The only thing he hadn't told Roland was the baby wasn't his, but that was only true for a little bit longer. "Don't listen to him; he knew. He's just trying to get me in trouble."

"Always," Roland admitted with a wink. "How's it working?"

Creigh smiled. "You're so bad."

"That's what Sharon says"—he lowered his voice and leaned in closer—"but between you and me, I think it's the main reason she keeps me around."

"I'm sure it is." Creigh laughed.

"We need to get together for dinner soon."

"Definitely." The pleasure in Creigh's voice warmed Dean's heart. He knew she'd always had a soft spot for Roland and his wife.

"Speaking of eating, I'm going to get out of your hair so the three of you," he said with a twinkle in his eyes, "can get back to lunch. It's been a while, mind you, but I remember exactly what it was like when the Mrs. was carrying. Don't tell her I said this, but she had an appetite like a linebacker."

Creigh laughed. "I shouldn't laugh, because it's so true. I feel like I could eat an entire slab of ribs with a large side of garlic mashed potatoes." Creigh's tone took on a dreamy quality that had both men grinning. When she noticed, she frowned. "What? It sounds good."

"Yes, it does." Dean bit back his amusement. "And that's what I'm going to get you." Turning his attention back to Roland, he asked, "Do you want to come with us?"

"No. I just finished eating, actually. But you two have a good time."

"I will." Creigh rubbed her had over her belly. "We're weeks away from liftoff, so I'm going to enjoy every last second of peace and quiet I can squeeze out until then."

"Weeks away. Already?" Roland's eyes widened. "Oh boy."

"No." Dean grinned. "Oh girl."

His comment caused the other man to smile. "Another girl. Dean, my friend, I don't know whether to congratulate you or commiserate with you. If this one looks anything like Harlow, you're in for a world of trouble."

"Tell me about it."

"Shotguns at the ready?"

Dean nodded. "All set and hanging over the fireplace."

"That's my boy." Roland gave Creigh a brief hug again before heading toward the door.

Before he reached it, though, Dean called him back. "Roland, before you go…"

Roland turned back to face Dean. "Yes?"

"What did you want to see me about?"

He waved his hands as if shooing away any concerns Dean might have had. "Nothing important. Come find me when you get back, and we'll talk then."

"Okay."

The older man gave a slight wave before opening the door and then slipping away. Dean wasted no time gathering his uneaten lunch and tossing it back in the brown sack he'd brought it in. "Let me go drop this off at the break room, and then we can go."

"Sounds good to me."

Arm in arm they left his office and headed out of his office. They were about more than halfway to their destination when Creigh drew up short and grimaced. Concerned, Dean stopped and looked down at her. "What's wrong?"

"Nothing," she said with a rueful smile. "I need to make a pit stop."

"Oh what, that whole twelve feet did you in?"

"It's easy to laugh when it's not your bladder being used as a trampoline."

"You're right." He grinned. "It is."

Creigh stuck her tongue out at him. "Jerkface."

"Yep." Dean pointed down the hall. "Bathrooms are right there," he said, in case she'd forgotten. "I'll wait in the break room for you."

"Okay."

Dean smiled at the cute picture she made from behind and waited until she waddled out of sight before continuing on his way. He didn't know what he'd done right to receive such a gift, but he was thankful for the second chance nevertheless. Not surprisingly, grateful wasn't the only thing Dean was feeling after being near her. He was aroused as well and counting the minutes until he could be alone with Creigh again.

Having her stop by unexpectedly like this was just one of those special little extras he'd missed in the time they'd been apart. Almost as much as he missed making love with her whenever the mood struck. If Dean had anything to say about it, lunch wouldn't be the only thing he'd be eating while they were out.

Dirty thoughts of what he was going to do to and *with* Creigh filled his head as he pushed open the door of the break room. His pleasant mood instantly evaporated when he caught sight of Trace, who was kicked back in one of the plastic chairs, feet on the table, talking to two men. The second Trace saw Dean, he raised the coffee mug he was drinking from in salutation. Dean's Father's Day mug.

"That's mine." Dean prided himself on the fact the words actually sounded coherent.

"Oh"—Trace glanced down at the cup, then back at Dean—"I didn't realize that."

Dean didn't believe him for a second. "Well, now you know." Not giving a rat's ass who was looking, Dean snatched the coffee mug from the smirking man, spilling a bit of the hot liquid onto his hand. He barely felt it, though, as the anger raged inside him. How dare Trace even look at his property, let alone touch it? Without saying another word, he made his way over to the sink and set the cup down on the counter, keeping his temper in check all the while.

Unfortunately, he was the only one keeping silent. "You really need to learn how to share better," Trace said from behind him. "It's just a cup, man."

"It's my cup," Dean said stiffly as he went to the refrigerator and set his lunch inside. "I don't want to see you using it again."

"It's not a big deal."

Dean turned around and faced Trace. "You heard what I said." Dean's voice was calm but cold. He wasn't joking around. Roland be damned, if Trace kept fucking with him, there was going to be a problem.

For Trace.

"Fine." Smirking, he stood and came to stand in front of Dean. "I won't touch your precious cup. Sorry if I offended you."

"You're not sorry, and there is no *if* about it." From the corner of his eye, Dean watched as the two men who'd been sitting with Trace shared a look with one another, then silently rose to their feet and left the room. Dean could just imagine the gossip about to be unleashed, but he didn't really give a good goddamn. He was done with Trace, and it was apparent he had to make that clearer. "I don't like you, Trace. I don't like anything about you, and you know it. But for some reason, you feel the need to keep fucking with me. That. Ends. Now."

"Look, man…" Before Trace could finish his thought, the door to the break room opened.

"I'm read—" Creigh called out from behind him. "Oh…"

Dean glanced over his shoulder to the doorway where Creigh stood frozen like a deer in headlights. There was so much he wanted to say to the other man, but this wasn't the time or the place. "Give me a minute. I need to wash out my coffee cup."

"Okay," she said faintly.

Dean moved past a surprisingly mute Trace and went to the sink. He dumped out the coffee from his mug, doused the inside with an abundance of soap, and turned on the hot water.

"I'm...uhh...going to head back to my office."

Dean snorted in lieu of answering. He didn't care where the fuck Trace went, as long as it was far away from him.

"I didn't...when did he get back in town?" Creigh question broke the silence.

Dean scowled down at the cup as he washed it out. "A couple of months ago."

"Why didn't you tell me?"

"Because when at all possible, I like to leave work at work." Dean rinsed the cup out, then turned it upside down and shook it a few times. "Besides, I can't stand him. He makes my ass tired just looking at him." Dean turned back around to face Creigh. The frown that had been edging its way into his features stilled the second he saw Creigh's colorless face. Ire instantly forgotten, he set the coffee mug on the counter and moved to her side. "Cara, are you okay? You look pale."

"I'm not...feeling so well."

"I can tell." Concerned, Dean pressed the back of his hand to her forehead to see if she felt overly warm to him. "I think we need to skip lunch and get you home into bed."

"I can't," she protested weakly. "The shop. It's my turn to close."

Dean could give a flying fuck about the shop. Creigh's health outweighed whose turn it might be. "I'm sure A-mei or the new girl will be more than happy to cover for you." Even if he had to bribe them to do it.

Creigh wet her lips. "Maybe."

"I'll call them if you want."

"No, I'll do it. I'm sorry about ruining lunch. I guess it's a good thing you didn't throw your food away after all."

As if he cared. "Don't be silly. The only thing that matters is that you and the baby are okay." Dean pulled her gently into his arms and hugged her. "I'm going to follow you home to make sure you get there okay."

"You don't have to do that for me."

"I'm not." He pulled back and looked down at her so Creigh could read the truth of his words on his face. "I'm doing it for me."

Chapter Nine

Numb, Creigh lay down on her bed and tried her best not to cry. She barely remembered driving home or letting herself in. Everything after seeing Trace again was a blur. It was as if his mere presence was a black hole, sucking out the oxygen and her ability to think into an abyss of nothingness. Damn him, why did he have to come back just when things were going so well?

Opening her eyes, Creigh rolled over onto her other side and faced the wall. She didn't think it was possible to feel any worse than she did the second she'd slipped out of Trace's bed. Man, was she wrong. Seeing him turn two shades of gray when he caught sight of her heavy with his child made her feel ten times worse than sleeping with him had. What on God's green earth had she been thinking?

Putting her hand on her belly, Creigh prayed for strength. What was she going to do? Dean needed to know. There was no way around the truth of that now. Trace was back in town. Had been apparently for months now, and from the look on Dean's face when she entered the room, still up to his old tricks of trying to get under Dean's skin.

There had never been a doubt in her mind the only reason he'd pursued her was to get back at Dean for all the wrongs Trace envisioned Dean had done to him over the years. And like a fool she'd played right into Trace's hand.

There were no ifs, ands, or buts about it. She had to tell Dean. If she didn't, Trace would, and in doing so would ruin everything good between her and Dean. Creigh couldn't let that happen. She'd foolishly pushed Dean away once. She couldn't bear for him to leave again. Not after realizing just how much she loved him.

The feeling of the bed dipping startled Creigh. Gasping, she glanced over shoulder and, to her surprise, spotted Dean sitting next to her. His suit jacket and tie were gone, and the first three buttons of his white dress shirt were undone. He looked a fair deal more relaxed now than he did in the office, but just as handsome.

Creigh eased up and turned so she was facing him. "What are you doing here? I thought you were going back to work."

"You thought wrong. I'm taking the rest of the day off."

His gesture touched her heart and made the conversation they needed to have even all the more difficult to start. "Dean, you can't do that."

"Already did. How are you feeling?" His gaze searched her face. "You don't seem as pale as you did earlier. Are you feeling better?"

This was it. A perfect opening for her to spill her secret, but Creigh couldn't get the words to slip past her lips. Dean had said he didn't care who the father of her child was, yet seeing the hostility that still existed between him and Trace made Creigh doubt his claim. It was one thing to raise the child of a faceless stranger and quite another to take care of a baby fathered by a man he despised.

Torn, she stared and said nothing.

"Creigh." Brows furrowed, Dean cupped her chin gently in his large hand. "Cara, talk to me. Do you want me to call the doctor?"

"No," she croaked out, finally able to make her mouth to work. There was nothing a doctor could do to ease her breaking heart.

"Then tell me what you need."

That part was easy. "I need you."

Dean smiled. "You have me."

"Promise?" She couldn't help but hope he continued to feel that way for the rest of their lives.

"Cross my heart."

"Then make love to me." One more time, she added silently. Once more before she ruined her second chance at happiness.

"But the baby—"

"Is fine." The only thing hurting inside her was her heart. "I need you." Creigh brushed his hand aside and rose to her knees. Desperate to feel his body against hers once more, she slipped her arms around his neck and pulled him to her, centering her mouth against his own.

Dean needed no further encouragement. Wrapping his arms around her waist, he held her to him and kissed her with a fervor that matched her own. His mouth devoured hers in a kiss so all consuming it left her dizzy and weak in the knees. But still she held him tight, needing his touch, his love more than she ever knew possible.

Just as she was beginning to lose herself in the heady taste of him, Dean pulled back and asked, "Are you sure you're up to this?"

"I've never been more sure about anything in my life."

Dean moved his arms and pulled away from her, breaking her hold on him. "I'll take that as a yes." He climbed from the bed and held his hand out to her to help her down.

"Take it any way you want." Smiling, Creigh walked over to him on her knees, then sat down and swung her legs to the floor. "As long as you make love to me."

Dean threw back his head and laughed. "I love it when you're feisty."

"I just love you, period."

Dean pulled her to him. "Talk like that will get you tied to me for life."

"God, I hope so." She said the words aloud, but they were also to herself.

Unaware of the war waging inside her, Dean laughingly smacked her bottom before releasing her and beginning to disrobe. She watched him for a few seconds, because as usual, the sight of Dean took her breath away. While she'd been spending the last few months increasing in size, he hadn't changed a bit. His physique was still as awe inspiring, panty dampening, mouth dropping as it normally was. Creigh could just sit back and watch him walk around nude all day. He was just that sexy.

Of course, Dean wasn't the type of person who would willingly give something up without receiving something in return. "Am I the only one taking things off?" Dean tossed his shirt to the floor.

"I thought you liked a challenge."

"Oh I do." He unbuckled his pants, then slowly pulled his zipper down. "Just not sure you're going to like my solution. I like that shirt. It would be horrible if something bad happened to it."

"Aww." She frowned, moving her hand quickly to her shirt to pull up. "Bully."

"I do what I have to do to get you naked."

"So I see." Creigh pulled the shirt off and tossed it down next to Dean's. "Happy now?"

"Getting there." He grinned as he pushed his pants down to the floor. "Your turn."

Creigh placed her hand on the top of her stretchy maternity pants but didn't push them down right away. For a split second, Creigh felt self-conscious about her baby bulge, an insecurity she hadn't been able to shake despite the countless times they'd made love. Nevertheless, she didn't duck and hide. Creigh had learned the hard way that trying to hide her belly was the fastest way to a sore behind. Instead, she took a deep breath and pushed her panties along with her pants to the floor and stepped out of them, then stood in front of him boldly and unashamed.

"God, you're beautiful." His husky voice made his comment seem all the more sincere. Whether she felt it or not, she knew he believed his words to his core, and that mattered more to her than a stretch mark or two.

"I bet you say that to all the knocked-up chicks you know."

"Only the ones I'm desperately in love with."

"Desperately?" It was satisfying to know he wanted her as much as she did him.

"Uh-huh." Dean walked toward her with a purposeful look in his eyes. "Sit on the edge. Then lean back on your arms and spread your legs."

From sweet talk to domineering decree, Dean was a man with many sensual sides to his personality, and she loved every one of them, especially the kinky ones that benefited her. Without hesitation Creigh did as he commanded. She was barely in place when he dropped to his knees in front of her. "What are you doing?"

"I'll give you three guesses." Dean moved his hand slowly from her knees, up her thighs, to the apex of her sex, where he used his fingers to part the dew-covered lips of her pussy. "And the first two don't count."

"I... Ohhh..." Her comeback was cut short by a gasp of pleasure as Dean silenced her with a lap of his tongue across her clit.

Fuck yeah. The first two definitely didn't count. Creigh closed her eyes, dropped her head back, and pressed her hips up to his waiting mouth. There were few things in life she raved about, deli-style cheesecake being one. But if she had to choose between her favorite dessert and Dean's talented tongue, Dean would win every time, hands down.

If colleges gave out a degree in pussyology, Dean would have earned a PhD by now. Not only did he use his tongue to pleasure her, he used his lips, fingers, and sometimes his teeth to bring her to the brink of madness. The man had skills.

In less than a minute he had her light-headed and aroused beyond belief. Creigh felt as if she were drowning under the weight of the pleasure he unleashed inside her. Yet as all consuming as it was, she didn't want him to stop. Not now. Not ever.

"Dean..." His name came out a hoarse, desperate cry. "Oh...God..."

So overcome with pleasure, Creigh couldn't form a coherent sentence. It was a feeling she was well acquainted with, thanks to Dean. For some reason, he possessed the ability to blind her to everything around her and make her focus only on him and the many wonderful things he could and *did* do to her body. And then she didn't have to concentrate on all the other worries that were plaguing her at the moment. He and his very talented tongue quickly and methodically broke through her barriers and had her spinning out of control, all in less time than it took to undress and climb up on the bed.

"Yes, yes..." Creigh surrendered to the pleasure crashing over her like a tidal wave. Tossing her head back, she tightened her grip on the quilt and held fast as she came, moaning her release through dry parted lips. The soul-shattering force of her release stole her breath and the strength of her arms.

Releasing the quilt, she lay back on the bed, dazed and thoroughly lethargic. As Creigh lay trembling in the aftermath of her orgasm, Dean pulled his mouth away from her tender pussy and rose to his feet. His mouth glistened with the evidence of her desire, and his eyes were as wild as a brush fire. "Get in the middle of the bed," he ordered in a firm yet husky tone. "And lie on your side."

As good as that all sounded, she needed a minute to gather herself. Hell her legs were still trembling. "I need…I need a minute."

"You have a second," he said in a voice that brooked no argument. "So make it count."

"Bastard." Creigh scooted back on the bed and placed herself in the position he requested. Closing her eyes, she steadied her breathing and waited for what was to come. A soft buzzing noise garnered her attention, and she looked over her shoulder. To her utter delight, it was Dean holding the handle of her favorite toy. "What are you going to do with that?"

"Anything that I want to."

Even if she wanted to, Creigh couldn't argue with that. When he was right, he was right.

Dean didn't know how it was possible; he only knew it was true. Every day he grew more and more in love with Creigh. Even now, watching her position herself on the bed, he was torn between two aches, the one in his chest and the one between his legs. Without much of a fight, his cock won the battle, which was more than okay with Dean.

It took a few seconds of digging around in her top drawer to find what it was he was looking for, but when he did, he smiled. Dean had been meaning to meet his battery-operated competition for a while now, and there was definitely no time like the present.

With the dark purple toy in hand, Dean climbed on the bed beside Creigh and spooned her from behind. Once in place, he turned the toy on and began to run it up and down her arms, smiling to himself as she wiggled to escape from the sensation. "From the way you're moving, I would think you don't like this thing."

"I like it just fine." She propped her head up on her bent hand and peered over her shoulder at him. "When it's used properly."

"Don't worry." He chuckled. "I know exactly how to use it."

"I'm sure you do."

"So tell me," he said as he ran the vibrating toy around her darkened areolae. They were even darker than normal, a side effect of the pregnancy, but one he didn't mind at all. Her breasts were more sensitive, larger by far, and just too damn tempting to resist. So he didn't. He used the clitoral toy to tantalize her pebbled peaks. "Was this my competition? Is this your Duracell lover?"

"Jealous?"

"I was. That is until your favorite toy and my cock came to a workable solution. They had a meeting of the minds, so to speak, and I think we've come up with a solution that will suit us all."

Creigh's lips twitched as if she was biting back a smile. "Such as?"

"Duracell will get your clit, and my dick your pussy. They plan to tag team your juicy cunt and then let you decide which you like better."

"It's going to be kind of hard for me to make that decision."

"Oh, baby." Dean pressed his straining erection forward and rubbed it against the soft flesh of her firm ass. "It's already hard."

Creigh moaned and pressed her ass back against him. "So I see."

"Think we should do something about it?"

"Yes. Yes, I do."

"Good. I was hoping you'd say that. Take this and press it against your clit." He handed the toy to her, and without waiting to see if she did as he requested, he scooted down just a bit and bent his leg so his knee was pointed up and his foot was on the bed. Then Dean angled his leg forward a little, then lifted her top leg and placed it over his. The move put her pussy in the perfect position for him to slide his cock seamlessly into her.

Reaching between them, he took hold of his cock and ran it across the damp folds of her sex. Dean wanted to make sure he was good and slippery when he eased inside her. Since they'd been back together, they'd been burning up the sheets every single chance they had, and Dean was adamant that she was not only comfortable while they made love, but that she enjoyed it as well. The second part was easier than the first, but for Creigh he had all the time and patience in the world to make sure he did everything right. Because at the end of the day, it was all about her.

"You ready, cara?"

"More than." She reached back and placed her hand on his hip and pulled him toward her. A sign as sure as any she wanted what he had to give.

Not one to ever be accused of leaving a lady waiting, Dean ran his hand over his cream-coated length to distribute her moisture evenly around his cock, then moved into position. He pressed the thick crown of his erection against the dark pink opening of her sex and eased his throbbing shaft inside her from behind.

"Ohhh...fuckkk!" he growled as the liquid heat of her pussy surrounded him, engulfing his cock in what had to be the only living proof of heaven on earth.

Creigh let out a deep moan and pressed back onto him as she placed the stimulator against her clit. "Oh...yeah..." Dean wasn't sure if the sound of approval was for him or for the toy, but truthfully he didn't care. If she liked it, he loved it. Whatever made her come was good in his books.

Dean lowered his leg a bit more so she was spread open at a more comfortable angle and placed his hand on her hips. Holding on tight to her, he began a slow but steady rhythm, easing his cock into her inches at a time to make sure she was used to it. But they were both too familiar with each other to be satisfied with steady anything. Wild was how they enjoyed it, so wild was how he gave it to her.

He picked up his speed and powered into her from behind, pulling her back against him as he thrust into her.

The newfound movements seemed to be just what Creigh needed because in seconds she was moaning, arching, and crying out for him.

Her hand shook around the toy, and he could tell at any moment she would abandon it. But that would never do. He wanted her to have the pleasure from both him and the toy. He wanted to watch her come undone under the force of her release.

With that end goal in mind, he ran his hand over the gentle swell of her belly, down to the sweet heat of her sex, and took hold of Creigh's trembling hand, hard at work, gripping the vibrator with all of her might.

"Allow me," he insisted.

She didn't even argue. She let it go, then immediately moved her hands up to her breasts, where she put her fingers fast to work on her nipples, pinching and squeezing the tips to give herself the little something extra she craved.

While she busied herself up top, Dean went to work down below. He switched the toy up to its highest setting and pressed it firmly against her clit. "Tell me how good it feels."

"Good, so good. I…oh…Dean…" She pushed back against him and away from the toy. But he followed her with the vibrator, forcing her to accept the pleasure that awaited her at both ends. And as he figured, it drove her wild. Creigh's cries of passion rose higher and higher as she began to really work herself back against him, taking him deeper and deeper inside her with every thrust. "God…yes. Right there. Fuck me."

"Like that, do you, cara?" he asked through gritted teeth. "Do you like the way my cock feels inside your sweet pussy?"

"Yes. God. Yes."

Dean ground down on his teeth to hold back the ear-blasting groan threatening to burst forth. She was so hot and so fucking tight that just being inside her was enough to make him want to come.

He thrust, over and over, with sure and steady strokes, all the while holding the toy to her clit. Even though it was touching only her, he could feel the vibration through the walls of her sex. He loved how it made her clench around him with every stroke and how the added stimulation drove her wild. The feel of her sex pulsing around his thrusting cock multiplied his pleasure tenfold and made it extremely hard not to let go and fill her pussy with his cum.

Dean began to feel the familiar tug of his balls signaling his impending release, and he knew he only had minutes left before he lost it altogether and began to pound into her like a madman. Picking up speed, he began to power into her with everything he had inside him. The bed rocked and dipped as they drove into one another, each stroke more intense than the one before.

"Dean!"

Her voice had a frantic edge, and he could tell she was as close to coming as he was. And if one of them was to go first, it would damn well be her. "Come for me, cara. Come."

Creigh released her hold on her breasts and reached behind her to grab his hip. She dug her nails into his taut flesh and cried out his name as her pussy flooded his cock with the creamy evidence of her desire. Her pussy contracted and spasmed around his pumping cock as she came, but Dean held strong, thrusting inside her until she came again. It was only after her second release that he dropped the toy to the bed and allowed himself to let go. With a low growl, he pressed his cock as deep within her and came, groaning her name.

It took a few minutes for him to catch his breath. When he was finally about to breathe like a sane person and not like a rabid dog, he made quick work of pulling out of her body and then lowering their legs back to the bed. Instead of getting up and heading to the bathroom to clean up, Dean slipped up behind her even closer and pulled her back against him.

"I really like the way you take me out to lunch."

Creigh laughed and pulled his arm around her. "Would you believe me if I said this wasn't exactly the plan?"

"No. Not for a second."

"Then I won't even try."

"Good." Dean turned his head and looked behind him at the clock on the nightstand table. "From my calculations, we have another two hours before we can expect the kids home."

"Two hours with the right two people can be a lifetime."

"I was thinking the exact same thing."

"We could always, um"—Creigh paused for a second before continuing—"talk."

"We could, but I'm sure we can find more lewd and lascivious ways to while away the time."

Creigh looked up at him and arched a brow. "You think you're up to it?"

Dean flexed his hips and pressed his damp cock against her ass. He wasn't hard right now, but if they stayed in this position for another two minutes, he would be. There was just something about her ass, her breasts—hell, Creigh in general—that made him act like a randy teenager. "I think that can be arranged."

"I was hoping you'd say that."

Chapter Ten

Creigh showered longer than usual, hoping the water could help wash away her sins and regrets. She couldn't do it. She couldn't get her mouth to form the words that would make Dean leave. She wanted to tell him the truth, Lord knew she did, but she couldn't shake the feeling that the second he knew, Dean would disappear, and Creigh didn't think she could take it. No, she knew she couldn't. She loved him too much to tell him, but she respected him too much to lie. She was caught between a rock and a hard place, and they were holding her down, ripping at her soul every second she kept the baby's father's identity to herself.

When the water began to grow cool, she rinsed off and stepped out of the shower. She grabbed her towel and dried off, then walked out of the bathroom to her bedroom and began to get dressed, all the while pondering what to do.

The sight of Trace yesterday had been like a hit to the solar plexus. Hanging around the house all night waiting for him to call had been almost as painful, but by morning she went back to the same revelation she'd come to months before. He didn't want anything to do with the baby. And that was fine. It was fine when he said it the day she told him, and it was fine now. The only thing that changed between that day and yesterday was Dean. He deserved to know. Telling him was the right thing to do. The only question was how and when. It needed to be soon, and it needed to come from her.

Yet still. It was far easier said than done.

Creigh was just starting on her hair when she heard the doorbell ring. Frowning, she glanced at the small clock she kept in the bathroom, surprised there would be a visitor so early on a Saturday morning. Setting her brush down, she headed back into the bedroom just as Dean walked into it from the hallway. "Hey," he said, closing the door firmly behind himself, "where you going?"

"I thought I heard the doorbell ring. Is someone here?"

"No, the kids were just playing. I told them to cut it out because you were resting."

"It's okay; I'm up."

"It's not okay; you need to rest. I still haven't forgotten about yesterday."

Neither had she, and the fact he was trying to be so attentive only made her feel worse. "Really, it's not a big deal." Her guilt made her words more brittle and harsh than they needed to be. She quickly turned her face away so he couldn't see her anguish. "I'm going to go finish getting ready."

She attempted escape into the bathroom, but Dean followed, stopping in the doorway to lean casually on the frame. "That's a pretty dress. Is it new?"

Creigh took a deep breath to compose herself before glancing down at the drape-front maxi dress she was wearing and smiling. "Yes, A-mei got it for me."

"I like it."

"Thank you," she said as pulled her hair back and clipped it up and out of her way. "It's so freaking hot right now, and the dress is so comfy and airy; plus it doesn't make me look as if I were wearing a circus tent."

"You can never look like you're wearing a tent."

"I don't know. The closer I get to the due date, the larger I feel." Creigh turned to the side so she could see her profile in the floor-length mirror. "The larger I look. These next two weeks are going to be a killer."

"I think you look beautiful." Dean walked over to her and stood behind her. He wrapped his arms around her waist and laid his chin on her shoulder.

Creigh leaned back against him and closed her eyes. "You're blind."

"I think I see you more clearly than even you do."

Creigh saw herself for exactly who she was, and she didn't like herself at all. She had to tell him. She had to tell him now. Afraid but determined, she opened her eyes and turned to face him. "Dean, I—"

The doorbell rang again, cutting her off midsentence.

"Damn it," Dean growled. "I told them to stop." He spun on his heels and headed out of the bedroom and straight toward the living room.

"Dean, it's fine." She hurried after him, not wanting the kids to get in trouble for just being kids. Besides if there was anyone who deserved to be punished, it was her. "Dean. Wait."

Determined to stop him, Creigh rounded the corner of the hallway, then abruptly pulled up short when she entered the living room and caught sight of a beaming Dean, standing with the kids in front of a room full of people. Balloons and streamers draped the ceiling in soft shades of pink and lilac, and there was a large duck-adorned banner with the words BABY SHOWER hanging on the wall. The second the guests caught sight of her, they let out a loud cheer and shouted, "Surprise!"

Creigh gasped and covered her mouth with one hand and her heart with the other. Although the rumblings of a baby shower had been raised by more than one person, Creigh had always vetoed the idea because she'd already had everything she needed, and it seemed sort of silly to have one when it wasn't necessary. Nevertheless, seeing all the people gathered around to celebrate the birth of her child brought her to tears. "Oh. My. God. How hard was I sleeping?"

"Hard enough," Gino called out, much to the amusement of everyone in the room.

"You..." Too touched to give her former brother-in-law a hard time, she just shook her head and looked all around the room at her friends and family. "I can't believe you guys. How long have you been planning this?"

"About a month," A-mei said, coming forth to give her a hug. "I know you said you didn't want one, but as usual, no one listens to you."

"So I see." A laughing Creigh was pulled from A-mei's arms into her mother's, then a neighbor's from down the street, then a cousin's. It went on and on like that for a good minute as friends and family embraced her, one after the other, and wished her well.

After greeting almost everyone in the house, Dean and the kids finally made their way over to her.

"So were you surprised?" Harlow asked, all smiles, as was Hamilton, who was surprisingly fatigue free.

"Yeah, Mom, were you?" he asked, hopping up and down to garner her attention. "Did we fool you?"

Creigh placed an arm around each of her kids' shoulders and pulled them in close for a hug. "Definitely. I'm so surprised." Creigh looked over to Dean and shook her head lightly. He'd done the impossible and not only kept the party a complete secret, but also executed the decorating and arrival of the guests all while she was in the other room. It was unheard of. No wonder he'd told her to take her time this morning when he slipped out of bed at seven.

In awe, she asked him, "How did you do all this?"

"I have skills you've never seen," he teased. "Besides, you know us De Lucas. We like a good party, and there was no way I was going to let any child of mine enter this world without a big blowout."

Child of his. God, she didn't deserve him, but she was going to keep him nevertheless. Releasing the kids, she reached up and wrapped her arms around his neck. She closed her eyes and let her tears fall freely as she hugged him with all her might, doing her best to let him know, in whatever way possible, how much he meant to her. The room erupted in a chorus of "aahs" and wolf whistles, which embarrassed her a little bit and caused her to bury her head in his neck.

"Okay, people!" Hamilton yelled. "Nothing to see here. Keep it moving."

Her son's antics, as usual, made Creigh laugh. Amusement overrode embarrassment. Raising her head, she pulled back a bit and looked up at Dean. "That's your son."

"Don't blame me." Dean reached out and ruffled Hamilton's hair. "Blame Gino. Kid inherited his big mouth from his uncle."

"Hey now," Gino called out. "I resemble that remark, as does everyone else in this room."

Gino's comment set off a round of smart-ass replies, which started the ball rolling in the never-ending smack-talking fest of the De Lucases versus Gibbses. Their families had known each other for many years, and the only thing they liked doing better than eating with one another was ribbing one another.

Whenever their families came together, it was a madhouse. It was all in good fun, of course, but it was wild—and loud. Over the years, after watching the way both families behaved, Creigh was convinced Italian Americans and African Americans were cut from the same boisterous cloth. Sure they had their differences, as every race did, but they also shared a common love for good food, great conversations, and family.

As soon as the party started, the group instantly divided, with the men going outside to bicker about the proper way to run the grill and the women moving to the family room to start on the sea of presents. Creigh sat in a chair near the fireplace that served as the place of honor as gift after gift was brought in and piled in front of her.

It took her almost two hours to open all the gifts and thank everyone for the bounty now stacked in the corner on the coffee table. There were more diapers and clothing than any one child could go through in a lifetime, but Creigh was ever so grateful to receive them. Thinking back now, she couldn't fathom why she'd been against a baby shower. Not only had she made out like a bandit, she'd had a great time to boot.

By midafternoon Creigh was exhausted. She couldn't remember the last time she'd eaten as well or laughed as hard or made so many trips to the bathroom. It was in the midst of coming back into the living room from one such excursion she caught sight of Dean standing in the open doorway leading to the front yard, signing a form on a clipboard. She'd barely made it to his side as the mail carrier handed him a thick letter.

"What is it?" she asked as he shut the door.

Dean shrugged and handed her the envelope. "Some downtown law firm. The shop isn't being sued for a bad flower delivery or something, are they?"

His attempt at a joke fell flat. That was the last thing she needed. "Lord, I hope not." Nervous, Creigh ripped open the envelope and pulled out the sheaves of paper. She quickly glanced through the pile to grasp what she was holding. There was a letter on top of a bunch of documents, with arrows pointing to where she was to sign, addressed to her from someone she'd never heard of.

"What's it about?" Dean stepped closer and peered down at the paperwork as well.

"I don't know." Creigh put them back in order and began to scan the documents again. It only took reading the first paragraph to get the gist of it all. Unfortunately, it only took Dean the same amount of time to do the same.

Before she could offer up any explanation, he snatched the papers out of her hand and turned them so they were facing him. It took only a few seconds for him to reread the damning evidence, but when he looked up at her, there was fire in his eyes. "Is this a fucking joke?" His voice was low, but the heat in his words rang out loud and clear.

"I...I..." Any sort of explanation escaped her. She was just as floored as he was by the document before him. This isn't how it was supposed to happen. This wasn't how she'd wanted him to find out. Not like this. Not this way.

"You what?" he growled.

"I..." Blood roared in her ears, and her heart pounded like mad. It took everything in her to force the truth past her dry lips. "No. It's not a joke."

The color rushed from Dean's face. "Trace. The father is Trace."

Creigh let out a harsh and painful breath. "Yes." And inside she died a little. "Yes, he is."

The silence that followed her announcement was explosive. Dean felt sick. It literally felt as if a vortex had opened and sucked all the air from the room. Dean couldn't breathe. He couldn't think. He couldn't speak. All he could do was feel. Pain. She... With Trace of all people. For a long, terrible moment, he thought it was a really, really bad joke, but then he looked at her ashen face and knew the truth. The documents weren't the joke. He was.

His sweet Baby H. The child he'd come to love and accept all without knowing her was the daughter of the man Dean wouldn't piss on if Trace were on fire. How was this fucking possible? Needing proof he hadn't gone completely mad, Dean looked down at the letter and read it for the third time, taking in every condescending line of the letter the coward had his lawyer pen to Creigh.

It wasn't just any letter. No. Trace, that motherfucker, was requesting a DNA test. An insult Dean took personally. Creigh wasn't a liar. If she said Trace was the only man she'd slept with, then Dean believed her, and he took it as a personal slight Trace didn't. Then to add insult to injury, according to the letter from Trace's lawyer, if the test determined he was the father, Trace would waive his paternal rights and make a onetime payment of fifty thousand dollars to go toward the rearing of the child. In return he expected her to sign an agreement not to request further compensation nor disclose his role in the paternity of her child.

He was buying his way out of his paternal responsibility. As if money could teach a kid to tie his shoe, to hit a ball, or could wipe away the tears brought on by a scratch on the knee. Dean always thought that it would take a piece of shit to walk away from a pregnant woman. Now he knew he was right.

"Dean." Creigh reached out and tried to touch his hand, but he flinched and moved out of the way. Creigh inhaled sharply, but his rebuke didn't stop her from speaking. "Talk to me. You're not saying anything."

"Might have to do with the fact I honestly don't know what the hell to say." Dean folded the papers back together so they fit with ease in one hand. It gave him something to squeeze, something to take his frustration out on, because Lord knew, no matter how angry he was at Creigh, he'd rather die than touch her in anger. "I mean I got nothing."

"Say whatever you feel." She stepped closer. "Tell me what you're thinking."

"I'm thinking you fucked him." Just saying the words caused his stomach to sour.

"Yes, I did." He stood there for a moment, waiting for something, an apology, an explanation that would make some sort of sense, but she gave him nothing. Just her level stare. It was more than he could bear. "Talk to me."

"No." This wasn't going to work. He couldn't have this conversation like this, quietly and calmly, with people walking about. All he wanted to do was scream, to yell at the skies for the disservice they'd done to him, and he couldn't do that here. With her staring at him with eyes begging him to understand. He couldn't understand. Not now, possibly not ever. "I need some air."

Shaken, Dean opened the door and walked out of the house. Unfortunately for him, Creigh was right on his trail. She slammed the door behind her, then went after him, down the steps and across the lawn. Before he could reach the sidewalk, she grabbed his arm and spun him around.

"Are you seriously just going to leave? You don't want to talk about this? Not at all?"

Dean snatched his arm free. "This is all I've wanted to talk about for months, but you refused. *You refused*," he reiterated angrily. "And now I know why."

"No, you don't know why. You just think you do. You have to let me explain."

"No, I don't." He stepped back, shaking his head. "Go back in the house. Enjoy your party."

Her temper flared at his command. "No."

"I need some space. I need to process this."

"No, you *want* some space, but you need to listen to me and let me explain what happened."

Dean held his arms wide, surprised she thought anything she could say would make this better. "How can you possible think anything can explain what you did?"

Instead of answering his question, she fired off one of her own. "You said it didn't matter who the father was."

Dean frowned, taken aback. "It doesn't."

"Then what's the problem?"

Dean refused to be made into the bad guy here. "You know what the problem is. You know why I'm upset. You..." Dean stopped and took a deep a breath. "You slept with him. Trace of all people. I think I would have preferred it had been one of my brothers. At least then I could look at you and not see the man I despised."

Creigh took a step back and placed a hand her belly. "Then I guess it is best you found out now and not when the baby was born. I would have hated for you to look at her and only see Trace."

"This. Is. Not. About. The. Baby." He bit the words out in an attempt to stifle the scream behind them. "This is about you. She can't help where she came from. I told you once and I'll tell you again. She's yours, and that's all I need to know in order to love her."

"And what about me, Dean? What do you need to know about me so you can love me?"

"I already love you. I'm just mad as hell. And hurt. You knew this would hurt me."

"Yes. That was the point."

The honesty in her words set him back. "Excuse me?"

She snorted in a show of disgust at him. "Do you want to hear it now?"

"Yes, I do."

"The whole point was petty and to hurt you, and do you know why?"

"No."

"Because two weeks before Trace came back into town, I drove by your house to ask you for forgiveness, to see if we could work it out, and you were"—she paused as if gathering her courage to continue—"opening the car door for some half-dressed tramp who was kissing you and hugging you. The two of you practically fucked on the trunk of your car. I sat there watching for some sick reason, hating myself, hating you, and I wanted to do something to make me feel better."

"So you fucked him."

"Not right away, but yeah, I did. We ran into each other one night; he brought up the divorce and made a pass. I remember thinking, 'What a dick. No wonder you didn't like him.' Then it hit me. Here he was."

"So you fucked him to get back at me?"

"I slept with him when I buried our marriage once and for all. I took cold comfort in the arms of a spoiled little rich boy who'd been trying to get down my pants for years. It was once, it was unmemorable, and I regretted it instantly. Not just the deed, but knowing I lowered myself, my standards, to get a revenge I knew I would never tell you about. I knew Trace wouldn't either. He's the type that would just love knowing he knew and you didn't."

That was exactly the type he was. And from the shit he'd been doing since he was back, Dean knew something was up with him. The way Trace went out of his way lately to antagonize him all made sense now.

"Now you know the truth. You can stop wondering. I can stop hiding, and we can both stop pretending this was ever going to work out."

Before he could reply, she turned on her heels and rushed back toward the house.

"Son of a bitch," he muttered harshly. Disgusted, he got into his car and roared off.

Despite what Creigh said, he hadn't been pretending, and it pissed him off even more that she would imply he was. Dean loved her, and he wanted to spend the rest of his life with her, but even he had his breaking point. After the bombshell she'd just dropped on him, he needed space and time to think, but more importantly, he needed to get his hands on Trace.

* * *

Storming off was bad, but it beat the dickens out of taking Creigh over his lap and tanning her ass. Even now that he'd had a time to cool down, Dean knew he couldn't go back and risk seeing Creigh until he'd worked out what it was he was going to do. Instead he found himself driving around for hours on end. Aimlessly for hours at first, then with purpose and a particular destination in mind toward the end. He had to see a man about a letter.

The drive to Trace's house took less than twenty minutes. Long enough to give Dean time to think, but not long enough to calm him down. He was still just as mad at the other man as he was from the moment he'd read his name on the document. He was, however, done with being upset with Creigh. The drive over had given him the ample opportunity he needed to put things into prospective and to get a handle on his feelings for what Creigh did and why.

If he tried, he probably could pin down the night and the name of the woman Creigh said she saw him with that set them on this destructive path, but like Creigh, he didn't want to dwell on the past. They'd both done things neither was particular proud of, but unlike her, he hadn't been tripped up. Her motives for what she'd done were no different from the reason he'd slept with other women. The only difference was she chose someone he knew to wreak her vengeance, and he hadn't thought of that possibility.

He couldn't blame her; he didn't blame her for the decisions she'd made. He loved her, and he'd forgiven her for sleeping with someone back when she'd first told him. Now that he knew the name of the man, nothing should have changed. But because of him, it had. He'd lost his temper and blown up, and for that he owed her one hell of an apology. But that would have to come later. Right now there was a score to settle, and it had less to do with Creigh and more to do with their unborn child.

Dean pulled up next to the sidewalk of Trace's town house and cut off the engine. He picked up the offensive letter off the passenger seat and stared at it. He could feel himself start to get angry all over again. With a frown riding low on his mouth, he stepped out of the car and made his way up to the building. Every step he took fueled his anger even more, and by the time he reached the door of Trace's town house, Dean was beyond pissed off.

One hand clutched the folded and battered law forms in one hand, and the other pressed heavily on the doorbell. Dean didn't know if Trace was in. But Dean had nowhere to go that was more important than being here right now. He wasn't going to leave this stoop until he and Trace had a talk.

Dean didn't have to wait long. After he pressed the bell for a second time, Trace opened the door. He took one look at Dean and frowned. "What the hell are you doing here?"

The gall of the other man's bravado was infuriating, and it called to Dean's baser side. The side that didn't necessarily want to kill Trace for abandoning his child, as much as Dean wanted to kill Trace for having the nerve to touch Creigh in the first place. Dean was at war with himself. With his morals and with his pride. And unfortunately for Trace, the other man was about to receive a visit from both sides of Dean.

Without saying a single word, Dean balled up his fist around the documents Trace had sent Creigh, pulled his arm back, then sent it flying straight into Trace's smug face. The right hook to the jaw was followed rather quickly by a left hook, then another right that sent Trace stumbling back into the house and flat onto the floor.

"Mind if I come in?" Dean asked as he stepped over the man and into his home. "We need to talk."

"The only people we're going to talk to is the cops, motherfucker."

His words didn't faze Dean at all. "Do you really want to bring other people in on this, Trace?" The threat of Trace's parents finding out was just what Dean needed to squash the bastard's threat to call the cops.

"Takes a real man to sucker punch a man in his own house. You must have balls of steel."

"Gigantic. And if I were you, I'd stay right there on the floor," Dean warned. "Real man. Like you, right? The type of man that hate-fucks a woman and impregnates her just to get back at his childhood rival."

A bit of the anger seemed to seep right out of Trace. "Told you about it, did she?"

"Today."

"I figured it had to be recently, or we would have had this"—Trace gestured between the two of them—"conversation a while ago."

"The moment I found out," Dean assured him. "And don't worry. I'm not talked out yet."

"Fine. You're pissed. I get it." Trace sat up and gingerly touched his jaw. "Is that all you wanted?"

"Maybe if this was just about the two of you fucking, it would have been enough. But it isn't." Dean dropped the papers in Trace's lap. "Serving a woman in the midst of her baby shower is a bit low. Even for you."

Trace let out a heavy sigh and picked the papers up, not even bothering to look through them. "Didn't know there was a party."

"I'm beginning to see there are a lot of things you don't know. Like how not to touch things that don't belong to you."

"Be as pissed off as you want. But at the time she didn't belong to you."

That was the wrong thing to say. Dean bent over and grabbed Trace by his shirt and hauled him to his feet, then threw him against the wall. The papers that had been in Trace's lap now lay scattered on the floor like the rubbish they were. "Creigh always has and always will belong to me."

"Fuck, man." Trace brought his hands up between them and shoved, breaking Dean's hold on him. "The first hit I might have deserved, but I haven't seen her since. You've defended her honor. You guys are getting back together. Lucky you. I'm not making waves. You saw what that paper said."

"Yeah, which is problem number one." Dean took a step toward Trace, who flinched but didn't back up. "Are you really implying you don't believe Creigh when she says it's your baby?"

"Lawyer thinks it is a good idea. His goal is to protect my inheritance at all times."

Dean shook his head in disgust. Spoken like a true spoiled rich boy. "And what do you think? You know Creigh. You've known her forever. Do you think she'd come after you for your money?"

"Hell, I didn't think she was still pregnant. I thought she took care of it. It's what I told her to do."

"You told her to get an abortion?" Dean's incredulousness seeped into his question.

Trace frowned and shrugged his shoulders. "What? I offered to pay."

"And she told you to shove the money up your ass, didn't she?"

Sheepishness crept across Trace's expression. "Something like that."

"Idiot." Dean couldn't believe Trace didn't know her any better than that.

"Look, Dean. I tried to do the right thing here. I offered money."

"In return for her silence." It took everything in Dean not to haul off and hit him again. "This is a kid, not a secret."

"I don't want a kid."

"Too late. You're having one."

"No," Trace said firmly. "She's having one. Against my wishes. Well, that's fine. She knew what I wanted from the first day she told me. I'm not the bad guy here. I never pretended to love her or want to have a relationship. It was one time. And I don't relish paying for this mistake for the rest of my life."

"It's not a mistake. It's your child. Yours."

"No." Trace's tone brooked no remorse. "No, it isn't. You can hit me all day, and nothing is going to change my mind. I don't want kids. I never did."

Dean shook his head in disgust. "Over the course of time I've known you, never have I been more revolted by you than I am right now."

Trace pursed his lips before replying. "You're entitled to your opinion."

"And you really don't give a damn?"

"No. I don't. Maybe I'm just not built that way. I feel nothing when I think of the kid. Nothing. Even seeing Creigh the other day, all I thought was, 'fuck, she's still having it.' Fathers don't think that way."

"Humans don't think that way."

"I am human."

"But you lack a heart and any sense of decency that would make you worthwhile. Stay away from Creigh. Keep your lawyers away. I'll make sure she signs the papers."

"And the money?"

"We don't need your money. I can take care of *my* children without any assistance from you whatsoever."

"I'll put it in a trust fund, then. He or she can use it for college. I'm not a bad guy."

"Yes, you are." And Dean wasn't going to let him think otherwise just because he was willing to write a check. "Since by an accident of God you're Roland's son and second in command at the factory, consider this my two weeks' notice."

Trace's eyes widened with shock. "You're quitting?"

"Yes." The only other decision Dean had made that he felt more right about was his one to be with Creigh the rest of his life.

"What am I going to tell my dad?"

"The same thing I'm going to tell your child. *He wasn't cut out for the job.*" Dean turned to leave, then thought better of it and balled up his fist one last time and sent it flying with all his might into Trace's abdomen. Gasping in pain, Trace doubled over. For a second he hung in midair, suspended by Dean's fist still shoved deep in his stomach, before keeling over to the side with a loud thump and groan. "That's for the baby, you fucking bastard."

Without saying another word, Dean headed out of the house, closing the door and that chapter in his life. He had one more stop to make before he went back to Creigh's. Then he didn't plan on leaving her side ever again.

As usual it was easier said than done. By the time he had everything he needed, it was after ten and the house was pitch-black. Dean was thankful the house key was with his car keys when he stormed out, or he would have looked all kinds of stupid standing on the doorstop, ringing the bell with her baby-shower present in his hands.

After slipping inside, he made his way to the baby's room. With his elbow he turned the light on and unloaded the bulk of the gift next to the crib before sneaking out of the house again to get the remaining pieces. It took only one more trip before everything was in the room and the house was safely locked up once more.

Not wanting to disturb the kids or Creigh, Dean shut the baby's room door behind him and began to put together the bassinet that had been in his family for two generations. It had been at his sister's house, since she was the one who had the last child, but now that their child was due, it rightfully came back to Dean.

The original plan was to give it to Creigh at the end of the shower, but since he'd split before that happened, it had stayed covered up in the back of his car.

The sound of the door opening startled him. Standing, he turned and spotted Creigh in the doorway. She was dressed for bed, but the dark bags under her big brown eyes made him think she'd been doing more tossing and turning than sleeping. Without saying a word, she slipped into the room and shut the door gently behind her. They stared at each other for a moment, the silence a dull roar.

"What are you doing here?"

Dean stepped to the side so she could get a clear look at what he'd been working on. The bassinet had been a labor of love. It was only a gesture, but one he was thrilled he could provide. She deserved everything he had to give and more.

Her eyes widened, and her voice filled with wonder. "Is that the…"

"Yes," he said with pride. "I restained it to match the crib and bought a new mattress for it. A-mei helped me pick out the bedding."

"It's beautiful." Creigh walked over to the bassinet and ran her fingers across the cherrywood finish. "I'm in shock here. I don't know what to say."

"You don't have to say anything."

"Yes, I do." Creigh's voice was firm, but he could still hear the underlying pain. "Thank you. It means a lot to me that you'd let me use this."

"Of course you could use it. It's the De Luca family tradition."

Her smile, along with her fingers, slid away. Creigh took a step back from the bassinet. "I'm not a De Luca anymore. And neither is this baby."

"The first is a mere formality, and the second is straight up not true. She's mine, Creigh. Nothing you said or did in the past can change the way I feel about her." Dean stared at her, trying with all his might to put his feelings into the words he was saying to her. "Or you."

"You say that now, but just a few hours ago, you couldn't leave fast enough."

"But I'm here now." A knot formed in the pit of his stomach at the thought of her not accepting his forgiveness. "I was always coming back, cara. I'd always come back for you."

"For how long?" She scoffed. Her doubt was as evident as the sadness on her face.

"Forever."

Creigh shook her head in disbelief. "What happens if, God forbid, Trace decides he does want something to do with the baby. Are you going to be able to handle it, handle him?"

Dean looked down at his knuckles, which were a bit raw and red, and wiggled his fingers. "I think I can handle Trace just fine."

His gesture wasn't missed.

"Dean." Creigh went to his side and picked up his hand. She ran her fingers gently across his bruised flesh. "You didn't."

"I did, and I'm not even going to lie. It felt damn good."

"I can imagine. Lord knows I wanted to a time or two." She brought his damaged hand up to her mouth and dropped a soft kiss across his knuckles before releasing him and trying to move away. But before she could slip away, Dean snagged her wrist. There was no way she was going to do something so kind and caring for him and still pretend it was over for them.

"Well, now you don't have to."

"I don't need you to fight my battles."

Dean placed his palm on her belly, and his child responded by giving a small kick. The movement made him smile, and it just pressed home to him this was bigger than him and her alone. It was about all of them. "Who said I did it for you?"

Creigh closed her eyes, a soft look passing over her face, before she swallowed hard. "I appreciate it. But you can't keep me on this merry-go-round. We both need to move on and stop hurting each other."

Dean reached up to tilt her head toward him, watching as she opened her eyes. "I was a bastard. I admit it. But no matter what, no matter how mad I get, I would never hurt you or our children. And I'll never stop loving you. I don't know how and I don't want to. I love you, Creigh, and I want you marry me."

Dean dropped to one knee in front of her and slipped his hand in his jacket pocket. "Just in case you were wondering, *this* time is the real proposal." He pulled out the small black jewelry box. "I have the ring, the ache in my knee, and the pounding heart to prove it."

"Oh my God." Creigh slapped her hand over her mouth and stared at the small box in his hand.

Dean opened the box so she could see the white gold three-stone diamond engagement ring. "I thought I'd do something different this time. One diamond for each of our children."

Creigh bit her bottom lip and gingerly reached out to the ring. She paused midway, then pulled her hand back and shook her head. "Oh God, I love you too. But is it enough?"

She'd said she loved him. Hell yes, it was enough. "We'll make it more than enough. Marriage is hard, and we gave in instead of fighting for us as we should have. But we've both learned lessons from that. We don't walk away from each other when we're upset. We talk even when we don't want to."

"And most importantly," she interjected, "we don't have sex with our significant other's enemy."

"Mortal enemy," he corrected just so she could understand the gist of it. "Mortal enemy, cara."

"Sorry, we don't do that with them."

"See, lesson learned."

"Is this the part where I say yes?"

"It would be nice if you did. My knee is killing me."

"Might want to get to the asking, then," she encouraged with a stifled laugh.

"Creigh, would you please agree to walk hand in hand by my side through whatever remaining days we have left in the this wacky world? Will you promise to forsake all others before me, no matter how mad you get at me? Will you promise to love and honor me and make me breakfast at least once every other month? Will you—"

Creigh covered his lips with her fingers. "If I make that promise, will you shut up?"

"If you accept my ring, I might."

"I might isn't a yes."

"But it's a start." Like tonight, he added to himself. "A fresh new start for a new happily ever after."

"Fuck that. I'm a realist, and I think we should get some bonus points for everything we've already been through."

He tilted his head to the side and studied her. "So what are you looking for?"

"Promise me happily *even* after, and you've got yourself a wife."

Dean pulled the ring from the box and took her hand in his. "Cara, mother of my three children, friend of my youth, possessor of my heart, will you marry me and live happily even after with me?"

"I will."

Dean slid the ring on her finger and rose to his feet. He pulled her into his arms and lowered his mouth on hers. He kissed her tenderly, gently, a kiss born more of gratitude and respect than lust and desire. When he was done, he pulled back and looked her in the eyes. "So you will, then?"

"Yes."

"No worries? No doubts?"

Creigh shook her head and smiled. "None."

"And do you trust me?"

"With my life and heart," she answered honestly and without hesitation.

"Good." Hearing the words confirmed was more than he ever wanted. "What are you doing next Friday?"

Creigh thought for a moment. "Nothing I can think of."

"Great." Dean opened the bedroom door and gestured for her to precede him out of the room. "Pencil me in, then."

"Okay, why?" she asked over her shoulder.

"Because," he said, coming up behind her to give her a quick squeeze before releasing her and moving past her to their bedroom. He opened the door and slipped in, then popped his head back out and answered her. "That's when we're getting married."

"Married!"

Chapter Eleven

"Tell me something. Tell me anything to get my mind off what they're doing."

"I don't think it will be much longer, cara." Dean's hand tightened around hers, but Creigh could barely feel it through the drugs coursing through her system. She was numb from the chest down and scared out of her wits. She should have expected her unconventional pregnancy would end with an unconventional birth. Although cesareans were common in this day and age, it was still considered major surgery and frightening as hell.

Going under the knife wasn't part of her birth plan, but when her doctor noticed the umbilical cord had slipped, he ordered a surgery readied. He'd told her cord prolapse was uncommon but could be deadly, and that was all she needed to hear. Creigh gladly sat through the sharp pinch of the epidural and the uncomfortable pressure of the catheter being inserted to have her baby born healthy and alive.

"What's taking so long?" She couldn't see past the green privacy screen they'd erected, and she wasn't sure she wanted to. The less of her insides she saw, the better, but at the same time she wanted to be in the know. This was her body and her baby, after all, but instead of interrupting the doctor, who was probably rearrange her innards, she turned to Dean. "Do you think everything is okay?"

"Of course." Dean leaned closer. He, like everyone one else in the room, was dressed in scrubs from head to toe. His hazel eyes were all she could see of him, but they gave her strength nevertheless. "Everything's going to be okay. Just wait; you'll see."

Creigh wet her tingling lips. "Promise?"

"I do." Dean squeezed her hand with reassurance. "Do you feel anything?"

"Anxious."

The lines around his eyes crinkled. "Besides that?"

"Pressure, tugging. But that's it."

"That's good." Dean glanced toward the covered end of her body briefly before his gaze returned to her face.

"Distract me," she said frantically. "Tell me something. Anything."

"Have I told you lately how lovely you looked at the wedding?" As usual Dean came through. Just thinking of their wedding day brought a smile to her lips even in this tense moment. For a courthouse wedding, it really had been beautiful and very timely, seeing as how she went into labor three days later. "I especially loved the reaction of the desk clerk. I thought she was going to have a coronary when she caught sight of your belly poking up from the white dress."

"It was ivory, not white. Perfectly acceptable for second marriages," Creigh corrected. "And hey, beggars can't be choosers. I had less than a week to find a suitable dress that I didn't look like a beluga whale in. It was either an off-white sundress or a multicolored tent."

"Either way you would have been beautiful."

"Doubtful. I'll never forgive you for making me take wedding pictures this big."

"We'll take them again when our newest flower girl is present."

"Yeah, well…" Creigh gasped in midsentence as the pressure increased tenfold.

Dean leaned in closer. "Baby, you okay?"

"I…" She felt as if a heavy weight was being lifted from her body, and then she heard it. The sweetest sound to ever grace her ears.

The doctor saying, "It's a girl" was barely audible over the shrill cries of her daughter. From over the drapes, Creigh could see the baby, whose arms were flailing about like mad.

"Oh, Dean," she whispered. "She's perfect."

"Yes, she is. Look at her. Look at her." Dean released her hand, placed his own hand under her head, and lifted her up a bit so she could see the baby. Not that it helped much. She could barely make out the baby's features through the tears in her eyes, but from what she could see, the child was beautiful.

The baby was quickly taken to the corner of the room to a warmer, but that didn't seem to please her very much. She cried and cried, kicking up a fuss. Laughing, Dean lowered Creigh's head back down to the table. "Do you see that? She has your temper."

"Hardly. I'm far meaner than that." Creigh sniffed, looking from the baby back to Dean. He didn't notice, though; he only had eyes for one woman, and they too were brimmed with tears. "Dean," Creigh called softly. "Are you—"

"Perfect." He looked down at her, and all the love he felt for their child shone like sparkling diamonds in his eyes. "Just like our daughter."

She knew in that moment that any doubts she could have had about him harboring grudges were put to rest. This baby was his, part of his heart, part of him. And they were a family. At last.

* * *

It was amazing what a difference two weeks made. One second they were having a baby shower; two days later, they were getting married; and a week after that, they had a baby. Milestones every last one of them, all happening back to back to back. And now, standing in the office of his former employer, Dean was about to pass another one.

His last day. Not that he'd been working. He went out on FMLA a few days after they married, but he didn't see the point of milking the system since he had no intention of coming back. The only problem he had with quitting was the actual leaving. He'd been in Roland's office now for the last hour, just bullshitting. Even though he knew it wouldn't be the last time he saw Roland, it still was hard to leave. He'd finally worked up the energy to do just that when the office door opened and Trace strolled in.

The second the other man saw Dean, his smile fell away, and his gaze skirted nervously between the two men as if he were afraid Dean had come to spill the beans. "Hey, Pops, what's going on?"

"Just congratulating Dean here on the latest addition to their family. A pretty little bit of a thing." Roland slapped Dean on the back good-naturedly. "Thankfully she gets her looks from her momma and not her father."

The irony of Roland's comment amused Dean to no end. "I couldn't agree more," he replied, tongue in cheek.

"Sharon and I will have to come over in a day or two to see her in person. You know how she loves babies. She already had a tiny little quilt made up for..." Roland furrowed his brow. "What did you say her name was again, Dean?"

"Halla." Dean met Trace's gaze. "It means unexpected gift."

"That is pretty. Very pretty indeed." Roland said. "Are you absolutely sure there's nothing I can do to convince you to stay?"

Dean looked back at the man who'd been like a second father to him and smiled fondly at him. "Positive, but don't think you're going to be rid of me so easily, old man. You'll still see me around."

"I better." Roland stuck his hand out, and Dean took it happily. "You ought to run out of here, though, before someone comes in and tries to put you back to work."

Dean laughed. "True. I need to make my escape while I can." Dean gave Roland a fond pat on his arm. "Thanks again."

Dean coolly nodded his head at Trace as he bypassed the man on his way out of the office. He was halfway down the hallway when he heard his name being called. Turning back around, he spotted Trace walking toward him. Curious to what the other man wanted, Dean crossed his arms over his chest and waited.

"So..." Trace looked around nervously before continuing. "Halla, huh?"

"You should know; her name was on the documents we sent your lawyer." Even though he didn't want anything from Trace, Creigh had helped him see they couldn't give up Halla's inheritance just to prove they didn't need it. One day she might, and she'd be grateful her donor had at least done that much to help her out.

"I haven't really had a chance to check them out just yet."

"Take your time. Signing away all your rights shouldn't be a spur-of-the-moment decision." Dean didn't want it ever to be said they'd forced Trace into this. If the day came where he signed away his rights and Dean could legally adopt Halla, that would be good, but his job as her father had started the moment she was born. He didn't need any stupid document to tell him otherwise.

"I'd think you'd be happy I'm willing to do it. The quicker I sign, the less people will talk."

"Trace," he said with a sharp laugh. "I'm a white man married to a black woman. People are always going to talk."

"I meant about the paternity."

"Let them." Dean shrugged. "She's my daughter."

"Only if I sign those papers."

That's where Trace was wrong. "You can sign or not; either way, she's still mine. Fatherhood doesn't start or end with semen. One day you'll figure that out."

"You *really* don't care she's not yours by blood."

"Not at all," Dean said with all honesty. "And neither will she."

"You plan on telling her?" Trace seemed surprised by the concept.

"Of course." Dean jerked his head in the direction of Roland's office. "You should think of doing the same. Your parents have a right to know their granddaughter, and she has a right to know them."

"And me?" Trace taunted. "Think she should know me?"

"Eventually, when you're deserving." Dean went to head back toward the exit once more but thought better of it and paused. He pulled out one of the birth announcements he'd been passing around to his coworkers from his inner jacket pocket and handed it to Trace. The other man took it without comment and looked down for the first time at his daughter's face.

"Happy Father's Day," Dean said softly before turning and going on his way.

His cell phone rang before he made it to his car. He answered in midstride, not wanting to slow down until he was in his car. He was so ready to get back home to his family. "Hello."

"Daddy, where are you?" Harlow asked. "It's Father's Day; you're supposed to stay home."

"I know. I'm on my way home now, princess. I had to stop and pick something up from the office."

"Okay, well, hurry. Mom isn't staying in bed like you told her to, and Hamilton won't turn off the TV even though I told him he was going to wake the baby."

"I heard that, young lady!" Creigh yelled in the background. "I had to go to the bathroom. Sheesh."

"But Dad said—"

"Harlow," Dean interrupted before the "he said, she said" could get out of hand. Harlow was taking to the role of his enforcer like a duck to water, much to his amusement and Creigh's dismay. "Tell your mother to get back in bed, tell Hamilton if he can't listen to the TV at a reasonable volume, he should go to his room and give Halla a kiss for me." Dean smiled at the thought of his latest addition. "And tell her Daddy will be home soon."

Lena Matthews

Lena Matthews spends her days dreaming about handsome heroes and her nights with her own personal hero. Married to her college sweetheart, she is the proud mother of two children, three evil dogs, and a mess of ants that she can't seem to get rid of.

When not writing she can be found reading, watching movies, lifting up the cushions on the couch to look for batteries for the remote control, and plotting different ways to bring *Buffy* back on the air.

Loose Id® E-book Titles by Lena Matthews

For Love's Sake Only
Happily Even After
He's So Shy
Loving Lola
Season of Love
Soaked
The Blacker the Berry
The Good, the Bad, and the Naughty

The REDEMPTION Series
Co-written with Lena Matthews
Logan's Temptation
Steven's Salvation
Lily's Surrender
Helen's Release
Sweetest Taboo
Body & Soul

"Into Temptation"
Part of the anthology Wild Wishes
With Stephanie Burke and Eve Vaughn

The Blacker the Berry and *For Love's Sake Only*, in omnibus format, and *Happily Even After* are available in print at your favorite bookseller.

3 1237 00311 6630